D1594100

Working on Sunday

by Edward O. Phillips

The Geoffry Chadwick novels:
Sunday's Child
Buried on Sunday
Sunday Best

Other novels
Where There's a Will
Hope Springs Eternal
The Landlady's Niece
The Mice Will Play

Edward O. Phillips

Working on Sunday

A Geoffry Chadwick novel

The Riverbank Press

Copyright © 1998 by Edward O. Phillips

Cover and text design: John Terauds

Canadian Cataloguing in Publication Data

Phillips, Edward, 1931–
    Working on Sunday

"A Geoffry Chadwick novel."
ISBN 1-896332-09-9

I. Title.

PS8581.H567W67 1998   C813'.54   C98-932055-3
PR9199.3.P44W67 1998

The Riverbank Press
308 Berkeley Street, Toronto, Ontario, Canada M5A 2X5

Printed and bound in Canada by Métrolitho

for K.S.W. and J.J.T.

"That," said Mrs. Jarley, in her exhibition tone, as Nell touched a figure at the beginning of the platform, "is an unfortunate maid-of-honour in the time of Queen Elizabeth, who died from pricking her finger in consequence of working upon a Sunday."

Charles Dickens, *The Old Curiosity Shop*

He koude rooste, and sethe, and broille, and frye,
Maken mortreux, and wel bake a pye.

Geoffrey Chaucer, *The Canterbury Tales*

I

I have always detested exercise. I know that statement makes me sound like an indolent man, which I am not. Weather permitting, I walk nearly two miles to my office every morning and home again in the evening. When I was younger, I used to play a fair game of tennis, and once I even had a go at learning to play squash. The lesson came to an abrupt end when I swung furiously at the elusive little ball and struck my partner instead. Sitting outside the emergency ward at the nearest hospital while a doctor stitched up the gash in my partner's scalp, I decided the time had come to abandon games. Marooned in that fluorescent-lit corridor without even a stale magazine to help pass the time, I looked into my soul. Not liking what I saw, I began to think about sports and games, only to conclude that the time involved, not to mention the incidental expenses, made them a poor investment. That squash accident cost me several cancelled appointments and a bottle of Napoleon brandy as peace offering to my wounded instructor. I donated my spanking-new squash racquet to a charity auction and retired gratefully from the arena of athletics.

Over the years well-meaning friends and colleagues have urged me to join their health club or gym, suggesting that not only will I feel better, I shall live longer. I have refrained from pointing out that when I want to feel better I drink Scotch, and as for prolonging my stay in this vale of tears, I'd sooner not.

When I say that I dislike exercise I mean what I have always thought of as vigorous movement in a vacuum: pedalling precisely nowhere on a stationary bicycle; striding with immense purpose on a treadmill, only to remain forever in the same spot; and climbing imaginary stairs, in defiance of common sense and the invention of the elevator, to learn fifteen sweaty minutes later that one has walked up the equivalent of sixty floors. Pushing, pulling, lifting or lowering bars attached by pulleys to weights strikes me as not unlike those activities one is condemned to perform for eternity in Hell. Even swimming laps endlessly back and forth in lanes clearly marked by ropes and buoys in primary colours suggests desperation, the frantic activity of dolphins or orcas trapped in a confined environment.

The question might then legitimately be asked as to why, dressed in T-shirt and shorts, I was striding resolutely into the future on a treadmill, that metaphor for all seasons. I had taken work home so I could begin Monday with a head start, only to discover that an important file lay on the desk in my office. Having made the trip downtown I decided to stop by my health club on the way back to my apartment. Since I was already ignoring the ancient injunction against working on Sunday I figured that working out on the Lord's Day would not cause me to lose any more points on the celestial scoreboard.

Perhaps a more pressing reason for my striding manfully into nowhere came from the insistence of my doctor. Last year, to my dismay, my former doctor retired. For years he had poked and prodded my ageing body, with a two-pack-a-day cigarette in his mouth or smouldering in a nearby ashtray. He also drank Scotch, rather a lot. His creased and furrowed face was a relief map of mornings after. Women found him irresistible. He knew about my sexual orientation and shrugged it off as *Chaqu'un à son goût*. Once a year, after my late-afternoon annual checkup, we would go out for dinner and tie one on. In spite of his human frailty, more likely because of it, he was a true healer. His retirement due to failing health was yet another reminder of my own mortality.

I was bequeathed, like an antique chest, to his junior partner, whose character had been annealed in the crucible of the sixties. He is a no-nonsense, nuts-and-berries M.D. He smokes not, neither does he drink. And it must follow, as the night the day, that he is a fanatic about exercise. Our first meeting was not an unqualified success. He asked me about my sex life. Far too old to be coy, I told him. He asked me sternly if I practised safe sex. I told him I practiced the safest sex of all, total abstinence. (I did not feel it necessary to tell him about my earlier years when I practiced enough unsafe sex for thirteen lifetimes.) He asked me whether I smoked. I was able to answer no, leaving out the footnote that had I liked cigarettes I would bloody well smoke and bugger the consequences. Then he came to the big one: did I drink? Yes, I did. How would I describe my drinking? "Social drinker," I replied. "One might even say heavy social drinker."

"More than four ounces a day?"

"Much more. It takes me four ounces to get out of the chair and get dinner started."

That was not the correct answer, and I was subjected to a medically sound but still sanctimonious lecture on the dangers of drink. A shrill, subversive voice urged me to say, "Go to Hell!" but, craven as it sounds, I share the collective terror of doctors. This man did not have feathers in his hair or bones through his nose, but he was still a medicine man, a shaman, capable of changing the course of my life and altering my destiny. At the very least he would corner me into a trade-off for the Scotch.

And he did. Who would have thought that I, Geoffry Chadwick, born in the Year of Our Lord 1933, corporation lawyer of some reputation, would be spending a valuable Sunday morning striding energetically into nowhere instead of stretched out in my Eames chair, drinking strong black coffee and reading the *New York Times*.

I consoled myself with the thought that, exercise notwithstanding, my day had got off to an unusually early start thanks to the telephone. I had fallen into one of those heavy, almost drugged slumbers that often follows a restless night. Consequently, by the time I realized the telephone was ringing my answering service had kicked in.

By then awake, I plugged in the coffee machine, then punched in the retrieval code on my phone. A woman's voice came onto the line to say, "You have one new voice message." She spoke slowly and with extreme care, as though I had just stepped off a plane from Outer Mongolia. Pushing 1-1, as ordered, I waited for the message. An unfamiliar voice spoke.

"Either you have been out all night or you don't answer the phone on Sunday morning. I'll get back to you. Be assured of that."

An odd message, but certainly not worth saving. I pressed 7 to erase it and put the incident out of my mind. Fortified by coffee I settled down to work and realized I had left the crucial file on my desk at the office. Unwilling to fritter away a day I had set aside for catching up, I bowed to the inevitable and came downtown, stopping at the health club on my way home.

A woman wearing a grey sweatsuit came into the exercise room. As I was the only other person there she smiled a greeting before climbing onto one of the stationary bicycles. The end wall of the cardiovascular fitness area was covered in mirror, probably to make the space appear larger. Without turning my head I was able to watch her attempts to program the electronic panel, on which the rider is requested to enter the level of difficulty, time, weight, age, and sex. The first time I used the machine I wondered if I would have to enter my tax bracket and social insurance number, but onto the screen flashed the words BEGIN NOW and, good Canadian that I am, I obeyed.

One of the fitness instructors came in to make sure she had programmed the machine correctly. He is a wildly toothsome Italian-Canadian and wears shorts that, were they a silly millimetre shorter, would have him arrested. He has legs that won't stop, a killer smile, and a bum that causes me to think impure thoughts.

Everything was in order, and the woman began to pedal in earnest. Handsome rather than beautiful, I would have guessed her age at fifty-five-plus. Obviously she had come to exercise, not network, unlike some of the younger female members of the club whose bouffant hair, glistening lips, bare midriffs and lace-trimmed leotards suggest that they might be interested in a different kind of workout.

The green numbers on the treadmill control panel counted down their flickering seconds towards my goal of twenty minutes. Now it was time to work out on the Stairmaster, a pair of motor-driven pedals which simulate climbing stairs. The machine is even more boring than it sounds, but it causes your cardiovascular system to stand up and cheer. I put in my customary fifteen minutes, climbed the equivalent of fifty-eight floors, and wiped away sweat with the towel I wore around my neck.

The woman jumped down from her bicycle and came over to the Stairmasters, one of which carried a sign: OUT OF ORDER.

"Do you know how to program this machine?" she asked. "The instructor is huddled over the phone and I'm sure it's a personal call."

"Of course," I replied. "You punch in the start code, like this, then press the ENTER button. Now you punch in the time you want to exercise."

"Fifteen minutes, please."

"Your weight? I know it's none of my business, but the machine wants to know."

"One fifty should do it. So much for secrets."

"The machine won't tell and neither will I. Which program?"

"Manual. It's the easiest."

By now the words BEGIN EXERCISE had flashed onto the screen in red letters.

"Off I go," she said. "I'll pretend I'm visiting my daughter. She lives in one of those older buildings without an elevator, and, naturally, I'm always furious at having to climb stairs."

"I know the feeling," I said. "One morning I came here to work out and the elevators were down. I had to use the stairwell so I could get up here to exercise. It put me in a sour mood for the rest of the day."

We shared a companionable laugh, and I went into another room equipped with machines which looked at though they had been designed to extract confessions during the Spanish Inquisition. After working out muscles that up to last month I didn't know I possessed, I showered and dressed. Fortunately the locker room stood empty. It might be suspected that a middle-aged homosexual could well find the men's locker room a good place to window shop. Such, unfortunately, is not the case. Because of the hefty membership fee, most of the men who come here to work out are in my age bracket. I have coined an axiom for the middle-aged heterosexual in a locker room: the bigger the abdomen, the more outrageous the underwear. One of life's more dispiriting sights is that of a large belly folding softly over bikini briefs dotted with psychedelic flowers or scarlet lips and worn as a badge of virility. To see these merchant princes exit from the locker room in conservatively cut dark suits one would hardly imagine a pair of Day-Glo briefs shimmering under the generously cut trousers. I would be the last to quash an energizing fantasy, but the hard reality remains that these men would look far more trim in boxer shorts or regulation jockeys. Public display of the flesh is a luxury reserved for the young.

As I was still damp from the shower I decided not to wait for the infrequent Sunday bus and took a cab back to my apartment. The driver had his radio tuned to a station playing Christmas music. Sorely tempted to ask him to turn it off – I was hiring this taximeter cabriolet after all – I feared his striking up a conversation even more than enduring "Jingle Bell Rock." I sat glumly through the misadventures of Rudolph before my building came into view. Bing Crosby had just begun to share his dream of a white Christmas when I paid the fare and scrambled out.

I don't really enjoy working on Sunday, but it helps me to get through what has turned out to be the longest day of the week. Since Patrick died my life seems like a long, empty corridor. I know what lies at the far end, but I trudge along, day after day, doing what I must and trying very hard to fight off the apathy into which I could so easily sink. Patrick and I used to talk about taking early retirement when, freed from the inconvenience of working, we would spend the beautiful summer months in Canada and devote the winter to travel. We even talked of buying a place in the country. I really quite dislike the country, too many bugs and not enough plumbers, but Patrick's enthusiasm was so contagious I could actually picture myself pruning bushes and pulling up weeds.

How many times had I read that the first heart attack is often the most lethal. I learned that bitter truth the morning Patrick's secretary telephoned me to say she had gone into his office with the morning mail to find him slumped over the desk. I can take some chilly comfort from knowing he did not suffer, or linger, immobilized and resentful, at the mercy of machines. He would have hated the indignity. So would I in his place.

The crashing irony is that Patrick was the one who looked after himself, going religiously to the gym three times a week for a strenuous workout. He dismissed the treadmills and bicycles as too sedate, and worked instead on the resistance machines. He lifted weights. We had just celebrated his fifty-seventh birthday, but even allowing for the pouches and creases he could have passed for ten years younger.

It's curious how appearing not to look your age is considered a virtue in North America. I suppose the reason is that many people discount genes and look on a trim figure and clear skin as outward symbols of inner goodness. Using that unreliable yardstick, Patrick must have been almost a saint.

I have never bothered to explain that he did not die of an AIDS-related illness. Nowadays whenever a gay man dies the first impulse is to blame Acquired Immune Deficiency Syndrome, as if older gay men did not routinely die of other causes. There are many out there who think of an AIDS death as the wrong death, as though dying should be measured on a scale of one to ten, like earthquakes. Dead is dead, possibly a blessing for the person who has ceased being alive, but an emotional black hole for those left behind.

Christmas compounds the ennui. I have always suspected that anyone past puberty who enjoys Christmas is not dealing with a full deck. Such is the power of advertising, however, that it is almost impossible not to get caught up in the holiday momentum, like someone trying to go up the stairs after a hockey game at the Forum.

Over the years most of the people who know me have stopped sending invitations to the parties they feel compelled to hold during these two weeks preceding Christmas. Enough festivity is jammed into the period from mid-December to New Year's Day to last anyone throughout the rest of the winter. "R.S.V.P. Regrets" read the invitations, generally written on a Christmas card. Almost always I telephone regrets, using the by now threadbare excuse that I expect to be away for Christmas. The holiday season is the one time of year I would choose not to travel, jostling for space on crowded trains and planes with all those unfortunates who believe guiltily that the birthday of Christ must be celebrated in the bosom of the family.

Needless to say, the number of invitations has dwindled to

a trickle. To run into the hostess, whose eggnog, pound cake, and carols you have declined, on the morning following her festive gathering only highlights the transparency of the lie you told over the telephone. It was with no little surprise therefore that I received an invitation from Audrey Crawford for this Sunday evening. "Do drop by for a drink and a little buffet supper," read the invitation, written predictably on a large glossy card featuring a Piero della Francesca *Virgin and Child*. Inside, under the politically impeccable "Season's Greetings" had been printed: "Mr. & Mrs. Hartland Crawford." In an intimate flourish, Audrey had drawn a line through the printed name and written "Audrey and Hartland."

I did not telephone my usual regrets. Audrey Crawford is a woman who won't take yes for an answer, and I knew I'd get a lot of flack about begging off. I should know. We once had what is now nostalgically termed an affair. Nobody has affairs any more; they have relationships, just as sleeping around has been replaced by having sex. Affairs were more fun than relationships, with their *mise-en-scène* of maribou trimmed peignoirs, chaises-longues, champagne buckets, and, above all, secrecy. Relationships are brisk, efficient, and businesslike, their props terrycloth bathrobes, hideabeds, mineral water, and pragmatism. Nowadays only British politicians have affairs, not just affairs but passionate affairs according to the tabloids.

I suppose Audrey and I really had sex, but we dressed it up with the trappings of an affair. She wore her mother's peignoir; we drank her father's champagne. We certainly were not in love; I don't think we even liked one another very much. But opportunity came pounding at the door: she found herself alone in the family house for an entire weekend. Sin beckoned, and what could we do but obey.

Audrey would have been the right girl for me to marry. Wealthy and well connected, she was destined from the cradle to marry a judge, a surgeon, or a CEO. Her wedding to Hartland Crawford seemed more like a merger in which Pulp and Paper said "I do" to Banks and Railways. She and I have remained friends; once in a while we have lunch. If she considers it odd that I have never remarried she stoutly refuses to admit the obvious reason. How could anyone who has known her in the feathers, however briefly, have not become a confirmed womanizer.

Friday afternoon, after leaving the office, I had dropped into our overpriced local market for weekend supplies, when I heard a voice call my name. "Geoffry! Geoffry Chadwick!"

I turned to see Audrey Crawford, her shopping cart filled to overflowing, heading down the aisle at a reckless clip.

"Why, Audrey," I said disarmingly, "I thought you'd be in the country."

"Would that I were, but the septic tank refuses to cooperate. And I'm having my Christmas party Sunday night. I do hope you're coming."

"Audrey, you know how I feel about Christmas parties, about Christmas anything."

"Now, Geoffry, don't be such an old stick. There will be people coming whom you don't know, in particular my dear friend Elinor Richardson who's just moved back from Toronto. Her husband died recently."

"Matchmaking again, Audrey? Do you work on commission, or do you just get first choice of the wedding presents?"

By now Audrey and I had parked our carts out of the line

of traffic. Audrey and I are exactly the same age, but she is taking arms against a sea of troubles. Her ash-blond hair, short and crisp, looked as though she had been sitting under a dryer less than an hour ago. Over the basic little nothing black wool dress and a single strand of pearls the size of chickpeas she wore a mink coat so deep brown and lustrous it was all I could do not to reach out and stroke the sleeve. Eat your heart out, Brigitte Bardot.

"No, I'm not matchmaking. But I'd still like you to come. Extra men are always an asset at a party; they add an element of adventure. And Christmas does tend to be so horribly wholesome."

"If anyone is looking to me to supply adventure then she – or he – is in for a huge disappointment. Is all that food for the party?"

"Good heavens, no. I'm having it catered. All this is because the children are home for the holidays, with their appetites and laundry and live-ins. It's enough to give me second thoughts about motherhood as one of life's richer experiences."

We shared a laugh.

"Now, Geoffry, I expect to see you on Sunday. If you don't show up I'll – I'll place an ad in the Personals column with your phone number saying you have found a black-and-white kitten."

"What a coincidence, Audrey. I did happen to find a black-and-white kitten. The superintendent is taking care of the beast even as we speak."

The encounter having ended in a draw we went our separate ways, she home to feed her brood, I to feed myself. I did not envy her.

En route to my apartment I stopped in at a florist. Were I to send a plant before going to Audrey's party I would be saying thank-you in advance. Should I decide to pull a fadeout she could not accuse me of neglect. I decided finally on a large white poinsettia. There are no free rides in life, and the plant would buy me time until I got around to taking Audrey out to lunch. Choosing a card from the display, I wrote: "The six Nubians I had engaged to carry my litter are moonlighting as Santa Claus, so I may arrive in a sleigh drawn by eight French-Canadians wearing *ceintures flechées*."

I reread the message, thought of Audrey in her mink and pearls, and tore up the card. Taking another one, I wrote: "Audrey, Happy Holidays! Geoffry."

By bringing work home from the office, going to the health club, and taking a nap, I managed to get through Sunday until the shank of the afternoon, around half-past five. There was certainly a drink in my future, perhaps several. I hesitated. Did I want to drink alone, or with other people? Either way a drink is a drink, but if I went to Audrey's I wouldn't have to bother feeding myself. As the same strolling players migrate from party to party, *le tout* Westmount would be at Audrey's, and I could get all those good wishes off my chest in one evening. And, who knows, perhaps the presence of other people would take my mind off the fact that except for Christmas dinner with Mother, I would be spending the holiday season alone.

On the point of leaving my apartment I glanced at my watch to realize it was only shortly before six. I poured myself a Scotch, just to get the motor turning over. Raising my glass, I silently toasted my doctor: "Merry Christmas and up yours!" Then I decided to telephone Mother, who at this point would have eaten her supper and returned to her room for an evening of television.

Only recently, and with great reluctance, I had moved my mother to a nursing home. The housekeeper-companion who had taken care of Mother for years developed phlebitis and was forced to retire. She would have been impossible to replace. A French-Canadian *vieille souche*, she was loyal, dependable, and devoted to mother. For days prior to her departure Mother and Madame or both were constantly in tears. In a world where there is little enough caring these women had become deeply attached to one another; their parting was a death in miniature. To my immense relief it was Mother herself who suggested the time had come for her to give up her large apartment.

As luck would have it, a room had become available at the retirement home where I wanted Mother to go. In order to make the move less trying, I suggested we keep her apartment until the first of May, when the lease expired. If at any point she decided she did not like the home she could move back and I would hire nurses through an agency to look after her. In a rare moment of lucidity she suggested that solution to be both costly and inconvenient. She really would be better off in a retirement home.

When I told my sister, Mildred, about the plan, she naturally tried to veto it. Mother should really stay in her own apartment. Failing that, she should come to Toronto so Mildred could take care of her. I pointed out, reasonably enough, that such few friends of Mother's who had not succumbed to the Grim Reaper lived in Montreal. In Toronto she would be completely isolated. Besides, the trip itself might well finish her off.

Mildred agreed so readily that I was immediately put on my

guard. "You're probably right, Geoffry. I would be a great shock for her to leave Montreal."

"I'm glad we see eye to eye," I said.

"Geoffry," she began, putting a spin on my name that suggested something major was to follow, "what about Mother's apartment? I know you'll terminate the lease, but what about the contents?"

"For the time being nothing will happen to Mother's apartment. I intend to maintain it intact until I am convinced she has settled comfortably into Maple Grove Manor. If she is unhappy, then I will move her back home."

"You mean to say you will be paying rent on an empty apartment?"

"That is precisely what I mean. As for the contents, aside from a few mementoes of Father and a couple of pieces that have sentimental value, I intend to put the contents into storage until Mother dies. Then they will go to you and your children. Furthermore, anything I may choose to take will eventually go to the children at my death."

I could almost have smiled at the pause on the line. Mildred had girded her loins to do battle, only to find the enemy waving a treaty under her nose. And hovering in the background, its presence more vivid for remaining unspoken, remained the power of attorney granting me absolute control over Mother's property. Mildred marches through life with a chip on her shoulder the size of the Royal Ontario Museum. One of my major pleasures is to set her up for a massive confrontation and then, by making an unexpected concession, leave her floundering. I know one day God will get me, but it will have been worth it.

"Very well, Geoffry, you are the one in charge. But an empty apartment does seem like a frightful extravagance . . ."

"About which you will say nothing to Mother. Do you understand me? Nothing! She is jittery enough about the move as it is, and I don't want her fretting over the rent."

I don't often bring the big guns into position by taking such a belligerent tone, but when I do Mildred takes heed. The move went off as smoothly as I could have wished.

Carrying my drink into the bedroom, I dialled Mother's number at Maple Grove. Even though the telephone sits on a table beside her chair, it takes her a while to grasp the fact that the appliance is really ringing. After a while she picked up the receiver. "Hello?" she asked, faintly apprehensive, as though the operator might ask her to accept the charges for a call from Mars.

"This is your favourite and only son. I'm just on my way up to Audrey Crawford's for her Christmas rout, and I thought I'd give you a buzz."

"Geoffry! How you startled me! I was watching television and somebody on the screen was about to answer the telephone and then the phone beside my chair began to ring. I didn't know where I was." Since moving into Maple Grove, Mother has been drinking less than she did at home, but I suspect she has nevertheless cut a deal with one of the nurses to keep her supplied with vodka.

"Art and life merge, Mother. Are you going to watch any of the Christmas concerts?"

"Good heavens, no. One gets so tired of carols and Christmas music, especially *Messiah*. And *The Nutcracker*. It's a charming ballet, but I fail to see what swans have to do with Christmas. And when the little girl pricks her finger on a toy and falls asleep for one hundred years, I wonder what all those children must think. It's so depressing."

"They're probably wondering if she'll wake up before they have to go to the bathroom. Now, is there anything you want or need?"

"Not at the moment, thank you dear. The nurses here are ever so good to me."

"How are you coping with the food?"

"The meals are fine, but meal hours continue to be barbaric. Lunch at twelve noon, supper at half past five. I have to have my first drink while watching *Sesame Street*. Are you coming for dinner on Christmas day?"

"Wouldn't miss it for the world, Mother. Anyway I'll see you before then. I'm off to Audrey's, and I'm late as it is." The last was a fib, but as Mother lives in a continuous present it is difficult to get her off the telephone.

"Do wish Audrey a Merry Christmas for me. I went to school with her mother. We both made our début the same year. May wore white lace trimmed with pearls. She looked lovely. I wore white *peau de soie*, or was that at my wedding? I remember both gowns were white, but I can't seem to remember . . ."

"I'll give Audrey your Christmas message, Mother. Now if you hear a dial tone it will mean I have hung up. I have to call a cab and zoom away."

"Very well, dear. But, please, no presents this year. We're way too old for Christmas presents. And I have no way to get out to shop for you."

Abruptly she hung up. I immediately phoned for a taxi. Liquor flows at Audrey's parties, and I don't like to drive when I'm stinko.

I had just lifted my overcoat from the closet when the telephone rang. My first impulse, as always, was to pick up the receiver. It being Sunday evening, I seriously doubted the call had to do with business. A so-called personal or friendly call can drag on for minutes, and my taxi was on the way. For a moment I hesitated. Perhaps the caller was the same man who had awakened me this morning and left the cryptic message on my answering service. My curiosity did not flicker strongly enough to risk being embroiled in what could turn out to be a long-winded call. What was the point of an answering service if not to take messages? I locked the door and walked briskly towards the elevator. Fortunately, it arrived empty and I did not have to nod in sage agreement as one of the other tenants observed that it was unusually warm for this time of year.

II

A handsome stone structure set well back from the street, the Crawford house managed to suggest a French chateau tamed by Presbyterian austerity. A uniformed maid opened the door and a young man, a moonlighting student no doubt, took my coat.

From the spacious flagstone porch I stepped into a large hallway just as Audrey came through the living room door.

"Geoffry! So you decided to come after all. Lovely to see you. And thanks for the gorgeous plant. You really are very naughty, but it's simply stunning." Before I could duck she had clasped me in an embrace and bestowed a softly sibilant kiss on each cheek. Luckily she stopped millimetres short of the skin, as her mouth glistened with fresh lipstick. Tucking my hand under her arm she steered me towards the bar which had been set up in the space between the back passage and the stairwell.

Audrey favours black. This evening the skirt was elegantly gathered, the bodice artfully draped. She wore the oversized pearls and, in honour of the season, had pinned a brooch made to resemble a wreath of holly to the shoulder of her dress. Sneaking a closer look. I could see the spiky leaves were formed of enamel on gold, the berries cabochon rubies, no doubt a stocking stuffer from her husband. Hartland Crawford would not have been the first husband in history to purchase a degree of domestic harmony with expensive trinkets.

Holding a Scotch and water as my security blanket, I drifted into the elegantly traditional living room, Audrey having abandoned me to greet new arrivals.

On those few occasions I attend parties I don't mind arriving early. Far too old to play at sophistication, I have discovered advantages in being prompt. The bar is not crowded, and shored up by a drink I have a brief opportunity to exchange a few pleasant platitudes with my hosts. Once the surge of guests begins in earnest I can retreat to a corner to observe who is arriving while they are taken up with peeling off coats, shedding boots, and saying good evening. I can also check out my surroundings, already familiar in the case of Audrey and Hartland.

The Crawfords have wonderful paintings, mostly Group of Seven, badly hung and well insured. Still, to see those paintings in the context of a house gives them an immediacy which is lacking in the hushed and solemn atmosphere of a gallery. How soon the avant-garde becomes traditional. At the risk of sounding unfashionable, I really like the Group of Seven. They offer no threat or challenge. They do not enjoin me to stretch my consciousness or exercise my awareness as though I were on the mental equivalent of a treadmill. And they manage to make the remote and dangerous Canadian wilderness seem far more romantic and approachable than it is.

From where I stood near the fireplace, fortunately burning imitation logs which look pretty but give off no heat, I could see the large mirror in the hall to the left of the door. It is a beautiful object, the marquetry frame highlighted by medallions of Roman emperors. Audrey once told me that when she asks the mirror on the wall who is the fairest in the land, the mirror replies "I am." That wasn't bad for Audrey, who tends to be depressingly literal.

Hartland Crawford strode into the room and shook my hand vigorously, as though we had just been introduced. Tall, large, with a pink face and silver hair, he always manages to suggest he is on his way to a directors meeting.

"Well, well, Geoffry, glad you could make it."

"Me too. Compliments of the season, Hartland."

"Hope you're in good voice for the carols." He gave a Santa Claus laugh, ho-ho-ho, and left. I was relieved. Hartland and I have little to say to one another.

I turned my attention back to the hall. A couple arrived whom I did not know. They looked like show-biz types, not Audrey's sort at all. He wore a blazer with a foulard in lieu of a tie, and her décolletage glittered with sequins, like something from Frederick's of Hollywood.

Had I not recognized the two men who arrived next I might have taken them for security, so dark were the suits, so sober the ties, so self-effacing the demeanour. The hair, moussed and blow-dried to a fare-thee-well, gave them away though, as did the jewellery, gold bracelets with links the size of Life Savers. Audrey always included a gay couple or two at her parties, mute testimony to her grasp of the larger issues. We nodded and smiled. Later in the evening we would drift together and exchange a few bitcheries, but not until the party had gathered its full momentum.

Having by now knocked back my first therapeutic drink, I headed off to the bar for a refill, only to be cornered by Penelope Tait, a woman I have known since Sunday school. To borrow my mother's words, "Penelope was always artistic," meaning she dabbled in watercolours, played the piano badly, and replaced her dining room table with a loom. She had been married, but one night her husband stepped out to buy cigarettes and was never seen again. Penny's theme seldom changes, how difficult it is to find a gallery that will carry her watercolours or a shop to sell her weaving. Her current project was ponchos, and the points of her most recent creation hung down over a full skirt of flimsy flowered material which trailed around her ankles.

All that is ever required of me when I talk with Penny Tait is the occasional nod or sympathetic murmur. I watched a man spill the contents of a chicken salad brioche onto the handsome oriental rug, then absently erase the mark with the toe of his shoe. In spite of the claims of good manners, I had to cut myself loose from Penny Tait and her aggressive, plangent incompetence. On the point of cutting her off when she next paused for breath, I heard a voice at my elbow say, "We've got to stop meeting like this."

I turned to see a woman whom I did not instantly place. Stylishly if soberly dressed, she made no concessions to her years. Her hair was lovely, heavy, smooth, worn in a pageboy reaching to the nape. Best of all was the colour, a silver gray almost like pale pewter. Unlike so many of her ash-blond sisters she did not have to examine her roots each morning in the bathroom mirror and wonder if she could postpone a visit to the hairdresser for another day or two.

Suddenly the coin dropped, and I recognized her as the woman in the health club, the one who had asked me to program the Stairmaster.

"I'm sorry," I said. "I didn't recognize you with your clothes on."

She laughed, exposing good teeth which were just uneven

enough to be real. To my immense relief, Penny Tait, aware she no longer had my attention, decamped. "Excuse me, but I have to say hello to . . ."

"I'm Elinor Richardson," said the newcomer extending her hand.

"Geoffry Chadwick." I shook the proffered hand; her grip was cool and firm. "Do you work out regularly at the club? I don't think I've seen you there before."

"Not as regularly as I should," she replied. "You have no idea how inventive I can become when persuading myself not to go."

I found myself laughing. "I know just how you feel. It does take a fair amount of determination to leave a warm and comfortable home for the rigours of the treadmill. And in spite of working out fairly regularly I still haven't won the lottery, or been offered a cabinet post, or stumbled over a briefcase filled with bundles of American bills."

"Life is seldom fair," she said with a smile. "We will have to wait for our reward in the next world. For me Heaven must surely be a place of negatives: no exercise, no taxes, no cholesterol, and no clever Christmas presents."

I smiled, more amused than I let on, and decided I liked this woman.

As if conjured up by a stage magician, Audrey appeared at my elbow. "I see you two have met," she said, extending her arms in a gesture that included Elinor and me. "Good. I wanted to make sure you two got to know one another before the carols. When they're finished it will be time to eat. Elinor, I was hoping you'd pitch in with the singing. I remember you sang with the choral society at university."

"Carols?" repeated Elinor in dismay. "Oh, Audrey, I haven't

sung in years, not even for my supper."

"It's like riding a bicycle. You never lose the knack. Hartland will lead us; he loves his moment in the spotlight. But I want to be sure there will be a couple of strong voices to take up the slack."

"Colour me gone," I said. "I'm carol-singing impaired."

"But we need more men," insisted Audrey. "There are far too many women as it is. And Hartland likes to do "We Three Kings" with three men each singing a verse solo. Surely you wouldn't mind being one of the kings."

"Audrey, we all have our pockets of intransigence. I do not steal roasts from supermarkets. I do not feed squirrels or pigeons. And I do not sing carols. Besides, I'm the wrong colour to play an Eastern potentate."

"Geoffry, you are the limit!" Smoothing her dress over her hips, Audrey went off to recruit singers while Elinor went to stand beside the piano, looking not unlike a Christian about to face the lions.

I have yet to attempt singing with a group when the designated key lay within the mid-range of my voice. I am obliged to keep transposing, sometimes up, more often down, an octave, where I rumble around in the back of my throat and end up coughing from the ticklish vibrations. The host was already handing out song sheets as I escaped into the hall, where the rival faction of non-carolers had congregated, looking at the group clustered around he piano the way the Guelphs must have looked at the Ghibellines.

Safely out of the danger zone and secure beside the bar, I was able to see the living room reflected in the hall mirror. Penny Tait was seated at the keyboard peering at sheet music through shell rimmed glasses. Now I understood why she had been invited, as she looked even more out of place among Audrey's friends than the woman with the glittering décolletage. At a signal from Hartland she threw herself into the opening chords of "Adeste Fidelis." Her bombast seemed to intimidate the singers, each waiting for another to go first, like adolescent swimmers at the edge of cold water.

The group next launched into a rollicking rendition of "God Rest Ye Merry, Gentlemen," and it soon became obvious that the pianist had no sense of rhythm. The untrained voices would have been better off *a cappella* than hindered by the intrusive piano. Only Elinor appeared to know what she was doing. Ignoring Hartland, who stood in front of the fireplace conducting as though his batteries were running down, she managed to keep the tempo and pull the other singers along with her. Hers was a pleasant mezzo, and with the help of a robustious baritone she managed to guide the others past the holly and the ivy through the silent and holy night to the little town of Bethlehem.

Now was the time for the orient kings to appear, and three of the men were press-ganged into singing solo. Gold, frankincense, and myrrh were duly offered up with varying degrees of vocal success and much friendly applause. This would have been a good time to call it quits, but Hartland announced they would all sing "The Little Drummer Boy." Here the performance began to unravel as the pianist made the error of trying to accompany the drum refrain and managed to stress the wrong beats. By now the bystanders in the hall and around the bar had grown restive. Carols at this time of year are hardly a novelty. The group began to whisper, then talk openly, and by the time the Christ child had smiled at the little drummer boy, the melody was barely audible. Bowing to the inevitable, Hartland smiled a gee-wasn't-that-great smile and tossed his song sheet onto the piano, a signal the carols had ended. Audrey stepped into the temporary vacuum to announce food was on the table and would we all please help ourselves.

Singing carols is thirsty work, and nearly all the male carolers clustered around the bar for one more highball. Having replenished my drink during "The Little Drummer Boy" I moved out of the way just as Brad and Gary, they of the conservative blue suits, came up the basement stairs.

"Is it safe to come out?" asked Brad, the taller of the two. They were both so tanned and toned and buffed, so blandly handsome after the manner of department store mannequins, that I had difficulty telling them apart.

"All quiet on the Best Western Front?" inquired Gary. "We hid out in the family room for the sing-song."

"A wise decision," I said. "Audrey tried to conscript me to be a king, as in "We Three . . . " but I was firm."

"We three queens were not cut out to be kings. I used to dream of being queen, but the job was taken." Brad looked around. "Do we have to go outside to smoke?"

"I think so. Audrey doesn't mind, but Hartland takes on."

We moved through the porch and out onto the front stoop. Gary and Brad lit up, then offered me a cigarette.

"No thanks. I just feel like a breath of air that doesn't smell of Rive Gauche."

"If the cigs don't kill you the pneumonia will." Brad inhaled deeply. "It's freezing out here, but that's Hartland. If he's so rich why isn't he smart? Look into his eyes and you can see the back of his head. How does Audrey stand him?"

"She's used to him," I replied. "Habit and inertia are powerful forces after a while. And Audrey goes her own way. She's in control of her life."

"I'll say." Gary blew smoke. "She's going to turn up at the undertaker's already embalmed. I like her parties though. Who else today offers an open bar. How sick I am of eggnog, white wine, and sangria. All that acid stomach and no buzz."

I shivered involuntarily. "If you gentlemen will excuse me I'm getting cold. I'll see you at the buffet."

"How do you manage to stay so thin?" asked Brad.

"I chew, but I don't swallow. Please talk about me when I'm gone."

I went back inside where I could see Elinor still hemmed in by carolers grouped around the piano. I waited until she came out, having decided she would make an interesting meal companion.

"I'm a talent scout," I began as she came into the hall. "We're planning to open a Christmas theme park, for those who need a little Yuletide fix during the summer months. There may be a job for you, if you play your cards right."

"And if I play them wrong I get to be Mrs. Claus in red and white polyester? Before we discuss terms I would dearly love another drink. I haven't sung this much since my aunt's funeral."

"Here, let me." I reached for her glass. "Anyone who sings every carol deserves to be waited on."

By now the guests had begun to drift into the dining room with the elaborate, feigned indifference that suggests they were going to eat only as a favour to the hostess.

"Don't feel you have to keep me company," said Elinor as I handed her a drink. "You may want to eat, while the food lasts."

"Audrey's kitchen is a veritable cornucopia. Her food never runs out. And I took the opportunity of getting a drink for myself."

"In that case . . . I take it you've known Audrey a long time?"

"Longer than it is gentlemanly to admit."

"I've known her a fairly long time myself, but never very well. She was at college with my husband." Elinor smiled. "Perhaps I should be honest and say my late husband, thereby telegraphing that I am a widow, armed and dangerous."

It was my turn to smile. "I heard a joke, not too long ago, about a widow on a cruise ship. I'll cut to the chase. She sees a pale and interesting stranger leaning against the rail and wastes no time striking up a conversation. Under her relentless questioning he admits that he is just out of prison, having served a twenty-year sentence for killing his wife with an axe. 'Oh,' she says as she sidles closer, 'so you're single?' "

We both laughed. "Did your husband die recently?" I asked during the lull. Jokes have a way of bringing conversation to a full halt.

"Less than a year. That's why I moved back to Montreal from Toronto. My parents are here, as are my children. This is the first party I've been to since I moved. And you can relax, Geoffry; I'm not on the prowl. I'm really trying to get some momentum back into my life. I feel adrift and I'm far too Protestant not to yearn for direction."

"Would I have known your husband? English-speaking Montreal is a small community."

"Andrew Ross. He studied engineering at McGill, but he ended up in industry."

"I remember Andrew: ruddy, heavyset without being fat,

jock – or should I say he was a good athlete?"

"That's the one. But he mellowed with age. So did I. We married, divorced, and six years ago we remarried. I almost blush to admit it. Any woman who marries the same man twice shows a shocking lack of imagination."

"Not necessarily," I said. "Getting married is like buying a car. You're better off if you know what's under the hood."

Elinor let go a laugh that was both spontaneous and infectious. "I never thought of it that way. Perhaps I could continue the analogy with used cars, but I'm too drained by the singing. The first surge of guests seems to have thinned out. Do you fancy a little food?"

Whoever had catered Audrey's party understood the basic rules of buffet feeding. No thin sauces or gravies lest they leak onto rugs or upholstery, and nothing that needs to be cut with a knife. A variety of salads was backed up by lasagna, Chicken Cacciatore, and Boeuf Bourguignon, the latter well thickened with cornstarch. To watch the affluent guests load their plates one might be tempted to think they had just stepped off a plane from a strife-torn and starving African nation. After serving ourselves, Elinor and I looked around for a place to sit. To tarry at a buffet means all the comfortable chairs have long since been taken, and we climbed halfway up the staircase to sit, the lower steps being already occupied.

"I have to hand it to Audrey," said Elinor, as she shook out the napkin to spread over her lap. "I find the logistics of this kind of evening daunting."

"Audrey is a very organized woman. And there is no shortage of money. A fistful of dollars is a great asset when throwing a party."

"I suppose. But money aside, it takes a certain attitude to be a successful hostess. Throwing a good party is not unlike selling a giant office building or pulling off a corporate merger. You have to want that adrenaline rush which comes from doing something well. I can understand the feeling, but all of King Midas' gold would not turn me into an effective hostess." She paused for a bite. "No doubt you've heard of hostess anxiety. I suffer from the reverse, a kind of hostess anomie, or accidie. I am overwhelmed by spiritual torpor and wonder why in heaven's name I invited all these people to my house."

"Didn't you ever have to entertain for business reasons? Surely your husband must have fêted visiting firemen."

"Yes, indeed. I took the precaution of having large events catered. And I had a Scotch while putting on my makeup. It generally worked. I never made the *Guinness Book of World Records* for my parties, not even the social column. But my guests had plenty to eat and drink, and I let them entertain themselves." Elinor stifled a laugh. "I never suggested singing carols."

I took refuge behind my napkin. Chicken Cacciatore is better when seasoned with a little malice. "To be fair," I said, "the carols were Hartland's idea. I know from past experience he believes a party must have a purpose. Simply to enjoy oneself is frivolous. If he's not organizing the guests to sing carols he's either networking or taking photographs. It wears me out just watching him."

"It's the Protestant ethic. We don't know how to enjoy our good weather, let alone a party." Elinor placed her knife and fork together the way she would have been taught as a girl. "Now, Geoffry, if you will excuse me, I must go and have a word with my hostess. Politeness dictates."

"Aren't you going to have dessert?"

"No, I prefer to save my empty calories for Scotch. And you know what they say: 'Girls who eat treats / take up two seats.' "

She made her way carefully down the stairs between the seated diners, and I fell into conversation with the couple two steps below. She wore the sequined dress with the plunging neckline, so ruthlessly engineered that she managed to seem at once shrinkwrapped and bulletproof. Her elaborate makeup, whose most notable feature was a black line following the contour of her heavily lipsticked mouth, tended to hide rather than enhance her natural beauty. Almost immediately we fell into the lazy North American conversational formula of "What do you do?"

I confessed to being a corporate lawyer. These days belonging to that profession puts you a notch or two above those who slaughter rhinos for their horns or Kodiak bears for their gallbladders. She in turn admitted to running the records office of our local cemetery. She had sensational legs, the kind men used to whistle at, although I doubt her particular workplace is rife with sexual harassment. Her husband, he of the endlessly adjusted foulard, sold insurance to various prominent executives, including Hartland. This couple proved yet again what I have always believed: that those who wear costumes instead of clothes are trying to create a personality for themselves.

I excused myself by saying I wanted a bit of cheese. Having little taste for sweets, I do not find desserts a temptation, even though Audrey's display of cakes and pastries, their calorie count measured in triple digits, beckoned enticingly. However, Audrey generally produces a well stocked cheese tray, and this time around she had included a crusty chunk of Stilton, the cheese I would take to that hypothetical desert island. Shamelessly I cut off the best marbled slice and was just fleeing with my treasure when I ran into Elinor crossing the hall.

"What heaven! That can't be Stilton!" she exclaimed.

"Sinfully ripe, and there is plenty more."

"My Achilles heel. I virtuously avoided the desserts, but I'm a Stilton junkie. I'd even use a dirty knife."

I followed her back into the dining room where she cut herself a slice of the pungent cheese.

"You surprise me, Elinor. You drink Scotch. You like Stilton. But you're a girl, and girls, as we all know, drink white wine and eat Brie."

Elinor laughed out loud. "You sound just like my husband. He was an unregenerate chauvinist, and I never tried to make him over, at least not the second time around." She speared a bit of cheese with the point of her knife. "If you ask me, which you didn't, I think too much sensitivity is bad for a marriage. Today's woman claims she wants a husband to share things with her, one who helps with the housework and comes home early from the office to be with the kids so she can go to her pottery class." Elinor paused to eat, and I waited for her to continue.

"After a while something happens to these women. Instead of colliding with the hard, grainy, reassuring surface of a male ego, they find themselves trapped in the connubial equivalent of Cool Whip. You can see them in the supermarket. Their mouths become tight and mean. They take up smoking again after ten years without a cigarette, or slide into the sherry at noon, or start lying in wait to entice the postman."

I laughed quietly. "I wish you could see my postman. Talk about seduction proof. But I still hear the small but shrill voice of reaction. Trust me: your awful secret is safe with me." I paused to finish my last crumb of cheese. "I have just about used up my party manners. If I hang around I will be tempted to drink some more and start saying what I think instead of what people want to hear. That means my first hungover call tomorrow morning will be to the florist to order bouquets of apology flowers." I gestured towards the front door. "I see people are already leaving. Getting a cab on holiday weekends can be a chore, but I have a magic number. Would you like a lift down the hill? Or would you prefer to stay a little longer?"

"I think perhaps I'll accept your kind offer. Sunday evening parties are by their nature meant to end early. And I'd rather have the hostess say 'Please stay' and mean it than 'Do you really have to go?' as she glances at her watch."

"You and me both. Do you want coffee?"

"Never in the evening. My age forbids."

"Mine too. Even decaf gives me the jitters. I'll go phone for a cab. Now if I can discover where that student put our coats, I'll meet you at the door."

Elinor gave a thumbs up sign, and I went in search of a telephone.

After what seemed like an interminable round of good-nights heavily larded with seasonal wishes, Elinor and I found ourselves in the back of a taxi which, according to the driver, three other couples had tried to poach. Elinor told me she had sublet an apartment on Sherbrooke Street not far from the West-mount City Hall, one of those period-architecture castles that looks like a movie set for a Robin Hood epic.

"Well," I began, folding my gloves and tucking them into a coat pocket, "that was almost like a party."

Elinor stifled a laugh. "Female solidarity obliges me to defend my hostess. She did as well as anyone could for what was basically a Christmas singalong. And that group was far too sedate. For a real party you need the rootless: the young, the old, the destitute, the hugely rich, the criminal fringe, or those whose beauty sets them apart from the herd. In other words, those without a vested interest in the status quo."

"I confess I hadn't thought of parties that way," I said, "I mean as being the preserve of the disenfranchised. When I was younger I liked to party on a one-to-one basis. I never did go in for crowd scenes. The expenditure of energy is seldom worth the rewards."

The taxi was on its last run down towards Sherbrooke Street when Elinor suddenly turned to face me. "Geoffry, would you permit this liberated lady to take you out to lunch? Now, before you have an anxiety attack, I do not have designs on you – even though Audrey assured me you were Montreal's most eligible bachelor. I'm still in mourning for Andrew, if the truth were to be known. But now that I've moved back to Montreal I'd like to make some new friends."

"I'd be happy to," I replied. "I like being taken out to lunch, especially by women. It makes me feel like a remittance man. I must warn you though that I'm more expensive on weekends. If I don't have to go back to the office I generally have the entrée as well as the *plat principal*. And I drink heartily." I fished around for my billfold, from which I pulled a card. "Here is my office number. And I'm the only Chadwick, G. in the phone book . . . My, my, what have we here?"

The taxi had just turned onto Sherbrooke Street, and ahead we could see the flashing red lights of fire trucks squeezing traffic into a single lane. We drove as close to the excitement as we were able, close enough to see it was Elinor's apartment building which appeared to be on fire. Smoke poured in an undulating cloud from the back of the building. I paid the driver and we scrambled out. A group which looked like they could be residents of the building stood huddled on the opposite sidewalk. Elinor recognized one of the group and asked her what had happened. The woman wasn't entirely sure; a fireman had banged on her door, ordering her to dress warmly and leave the building. As far as she could tell, the woman in number 37 had put something onto a back burner and forgotten it. When she finally realized the kitchen was opaque with smoke, she panicked and ran into the hallway to pound on doors. By the time the woman had managed to summon a tenant who realized this was a real emergency, a fire had taken hold.

Fortunately, the fire escape led up to the kitchen door, which the firemen were able to force open prior to drenching the area with hoses. Even as we watched the volume of smoke began to diminish.

"I'm in number 35, right next door to the smoke, so she would have been out of luck knocking on the door," Elinor said. "I wonder if the fire has spread to my apartment?"

"When I was a lad Mother used to say that where there's smoke, et cetera. Maybe we'd better speak to someone in charge."

"There's no need for you to hang around," she said. "Why don't you go home and tuck in. I'll cope."

"Not at all. Look, there's someone who seems suitably official." Taking her arm I guided her across the barrier, where a heavyset man with iron-gray hair conferred with two firemen. "Good evening. This is Mrs. Richardson. She lives in number

35. Can she go up?"

"Not at the moment, sir. The fire seems to be under control, but we can't be certain it's completely out. These are old buildings, and fire can creep into unlikely places."

"Have you any idea when I will be able to get inside?" Elinor inquired. Standing about Sherbrooke Street on a winter night was not a tempting prospect.

"I'm sorry, Mrs. Richardson, but I can't tell you that. If you have some place you can spend the night, family or friends, I would urge you to go there. Now, if you will excuse me." He turned to confer with a fireman who had just emerged form the building.

"Well, well, well," she said as we moved away from the barrier and across the single lane of traffic, "not the way I had expected the evening to end."

"Even though you have sublet the apartment furnished, is there anything of yours up there you are concerned about: documents? jewellery?"

"Not really. My clothes are up there, but not much else. Such jewellery as I own I am wearing, and I keep any valuable papers in the bank. My problem is where to go. Do you know of a good apartment hotel? If I'm going to move, I'll want to stay put at least until after the New Year."

"Don't you have family in Montreal?"

"Yes, but nowhere I can be comfortable. My daughter has two small children and a love seat that pulls out into a very narrow bed. I could go to my parents, a recliner in the den and Mother tutting and clucking as she cooks a huge breakfast I don't want to eat. I suppose I could call my brother, but his sister-in-law is visiting from the U.K., and I'd have to share their Laura

Ashley guest room with a woman I don't know."

"Don't you have more than one child?"

"Yes, but my son has a pad, not an apartment – waterbed, duvet, chicks. I don't want to know. My friend Amy would put me up, but her son is here for Christmas week. That means she would insist on giving me her room while she slept on the couch. A hotel is by far my first choice."

"There is an alternative. I recently moved my mother into a nursing home, and until I am certain she is settled in comfortably, I am keeping the apartment intact. It's sitting empty, only a short walk away."

"That's very kind of you, Geoffry. And you have no idea how much I am tempted. But it is your mother's house, and you scarcely know me."

"That is not entirely true. I may not know about your imperfect past or indefinite future, but you come from the community. You have raised two children. Your parents live nearby; furthermore, you are on speaking terms with them. You don't smoke, and I believe you have enough native wit not to leave the stove unattended. I shouldn't imagine you will trash the place or decamp with the flat silver."

"With such an endorsement it would be churlish of me not to accept your offer."

"In that case let us be on our way. I'll have to explain you to the night security guard. And I carry the key to Mother's apartment with my own."

It can be interesting to see a house or an apartment with which you are familiar through the eyes of another person. The building from which Mother had recently moved was built at a time when space and elegance took precedence over efficiency.

The brass fittings on the oak door gleamed from regular polishings and it was evident that the handsome travertine foyer, with its working fireplace, had not been designed to accommodate a doorman and his security screens.

The night porter, a small man with the sharp, bright face of a ferret, looked at me suspiciously as I explained the situation. I could see him thinking that if I was going "to 'ave a bit of slap and tickle," why didn't I use my own flat; however, I have never considered the hired help as arbiters of my moral conduct. I told him to do everything possible to make Mrs. Richardson's visit as painless as possible; furthermore, he was to alert the man who came on duty at seven. As the Christmas gratuities had yet to be distributed, he did everything but tug his forelock.

We rode an elevator, whose walnut panels had been buffed to a rich gloss, to the top floor. Mother's apartment lay at the far end of the corridor. I unlocked the door and turned on some lights. The living room lay on one side of a large reception hall, a dining room on the other. In her younger days Mother had haunted auctions and estate sales, adding to furniture both she and father had inherited. The final effect, seen through Elinor's eyes, was impressive. Elinor observed that calling the apartment a two-bedroom flat was like referring to Versailles as a very large house.

Things did not so much match as blend. Porcelain gleamed, brocade shimmered, silver cast its soft glow into the reflective surface of polished wood, happily free of protective glass covers. Although everything in the apartment was choice, the furniture, rugs, and objects had been handled, sat upon, walked over. It was a home, not a showroom, an impression further enhanced by the faint, pungent odour of stale cigarette smoke and numerous ashtrays, a reminder of Mother's three-pack-a-day habit. Should Mother decide to remain at Maple Grove Manor, one more example of a possibly outdated but immensely agreeable mode of life would vanish.

I opened the door in the hall closet to show Elinor where to hang her coat. I also lifted out a hanger still covered in a plastic dry cleaner's bag. "Here's a bathrobe of Mother's. You may find it a bit small, but who's to see? The master bedroom is down here."

I led the way into Mother's bedroom, densely furnished with a Victorian mahogany set dominated by a massive four-poster bed. On top of the chiffonnier sat Mother's collection of photographs, her rogues' gallery as we called it, all in silver frames that were beginning to tarnish. Elinor crossed to look more closely at the photographs, then lifted one down.

"This must be your wedding picture," she said. "You really haven't changed all that much."

I looked over her shoulder, examining the photograph for the first time in many years. Most tall men look dashing in a cutaway. My contours were much the same, allowances made for the pull of gravity. Dark-blond hair had turned to gray. Heavy lines now bracketed the wide mouth below a prominent nose, and the pale eyes, blue in technicolour, were by now framed in wrinkles. It was a face seen in pentimento, as if thirty-five years of accumulated experience had been erased. Unlike Elinor, I found myself looking at the face of a stranger.

"Your wife is very pretty," said Elinor. "More than pretty, she looks alive. So many brides look a bit waxy in their wedding pictures, but she looks as though she was enjoying the party."

"She did, and she always came across as intensely alive,

even when she slept. I could not believe that so young and vibrant a person could be so casually killed in an accident."

Elinor replaced the photograph on the chiffonnier. "There isn't any good news about dying young, except perhaps that if a person you really love should die then the love endures. I imagine you will always love your wife because she died before love did. I'm glad Andrew and I had a chance to get together again. Had he died during our divorce proceeding I would always have felt a lingering animosity." She gave a nervous laugh. "My goodness, I am waxing sententious. You said there was a second bedroom?"

"Yes, where the housekeeper slept." I led the way into the smaller room furnished with a rock-solid maple bedroom set which must have looked vaguely contemporary in 1945. Above the bed hung a Victorian engraving of a Biblical scene, the Wedding at Cana, I think, although considering the aquiline noses and flaxen curls on most of the male guests I suspected a number of uncircumcised dicks lurked under the Grecian drapery. Father bought the engraving at an auction for the solid oak frame. Tastes in art may fluctuate, but a good frame lasts forever.

"I think I'll sleep in here, if you don't mind," said Elinor. "There's something intensely personal about a bedroom, and the larger room speaks of your mother."

"Suit yourself. Now, in the morning would you prefer coffee or tea?"

"Coffee, if it's available."

I led the way into Mother's perfect nineteen-forties kitchen, whose one concession to the passing decades was a small dishwasher. I opened the contoured door of the refrigerator and found a tin of coffee.

"I'm afraid you'll have to use a percolator. Remember those?"

"I last saw one at the Smithsonian Institute."

"Then I'm on my way. Here, you'd better have a key." I opened the top drawer of a bow-front chest in the hall and took out a key from whose ring hung a medallion of St. Christopher.

"This is an unfamiliar situation for me, Geoffry, and I don't know the protocol. Ought I to offer you a drink of your mother's liquor before you go? I saw the decanters on the sideboard. But you have not removed your overcoat, which suggests you may prefer to leave."

"Thanks, but I think I will. Tomorrow is Monday, a work day. Call when you learn the condition of your apartment. I'm generally at the office by nine. Sleep as well as you can under the circumstances." I smiled. "I have to admit I admire your cool. If I were in your situation I'd have to be lashed down and shot full of tranquilizers."

"What sustains me is the hope that the plum coloured suit I foolishly bought on sale last week is too badly charred to wear. Seriously though, Geoffry, thank you. Letting me stay here is on the far side of kind. A fire is unnerving. I suppose I should call the people from whom I sublet."

"I would, but not tonight. Get some sleep if you can. Tomorrow will be a long day."

Elinor followed me to the front door and waited until, with a wave, I stepped onto the elevator. In the lobby I paused to say goodnight to the porter. I did not care in the least whether or not he had a good night, or even a passable one. But he would be able to spend the rest of his shift wondering whether I was the fastest fuck in town.

Back in my own living room I watched a few minutes of television, a nightly ritual which puts me almost instantly to sleep. To sit passively in front of those flickering images, be they news stories, movies, or show-business types chatting endlessly about themselves, causes me to nod off far more quickly than any sleep-inducing medication could. Realizing I'd dozed off, I jolted myself awake, turned off the TV, and was just about to climb into bed when I remembered the telephone call I had chosen not to answer earlier. Should I let it go until the morning? Oh, well, I thought, why not now, and punched in the code.

On came the Berlitz voice to tell me I had one new voice message. I pushed the appropriate buttons and waited. "Geoffry Chadwick," said the voice which had left the previous message, "you are a hard man to catch. You probably won't remember me, but that doesn't matter. You'll remember me well enough when I fix you for what you did to me."

That was it, the entire message. The plummy operator's voice came onto the line asking whether I wanted to erase or save the message. I pressed 9 to save the message, then listened to my mystery caller a second time. My aural memory is fairly good, but I could not place the voice, deep and masculine; the caller would have sounded sexy had his words not held a threat. In disbelief, I listened one more time. Almost everyone receives random crank calls at some point or other, but this caller had spoken my name.

Uncertain of what to do, I did nothing. Late Sunday night during the holiday season is no time to report an unwelcome call. The overworked police would only be interested in a series of threatening calls, and the Bell business office would be closed until the morning.

As my law practice is carried on outside the courtroom, I have never been the kind of lawyer or prosecuting attorney who sends felons to prison for long stretches of time. The call could not have come from a disgruntled parolee working off a grudge he had been nursing for years behind bars. I am well aware that life is not a popularity contest and that there are any number of people out there who don't like me, but nobody I could think of would go so far as making threats over the telephone.

My first reaction was to erase the unpleasant message, but I paused. Should the situation escalate, the police would want to hear it. I sincerely hoped this contingency would not arise as I climbed into bed and waited uneasily for sleep to come.

III

Sometime after ten on Monday morning my secretary buzzed me to say an Elinor Richardson was on the line. "Put her through, please . . . Good morning, Elinor. Did you sleep well?"

"Much better than I had any right to. It must be my untroubled conscience. I made coffee in your mother's percolator, and it tasted just like coffee. Then I trudged over to view the damage."

"Bad news?"

"Yes and no. My kitchen is back to back with the one where the fire started. They share a common vent. Some hotshot fireman who obviously loves his job knocked a large hole in the wall between the two kitchens, presumably to make sure the fire hadn't spread. All that heavy black smoke came billowing into my apartment and covered everything with a layer of greasy soot. The smell is overpowering. The place is theoretically habitable, but I don't want to touch anything before the real tenants have a chance to deal with their insurance company. I may just move into an apartment hotel until after New Year's Day. I had planned to start looking for something permanent after the holidays, so perhaps it's just as well."

I could not resist a chuckle. "One of the qualities I have always admired about my countrymen, sorry, countrypersons, is their capacity for turning unmitigated disaster into a disguised blessing. As evidence I offer those frightful photocopied letters some people include with their Christmas cards. 'Dear friends, we smashed up the car, but it needed a new muffler, and now we won't have to bother. Aunt Edna fell down the cellar stairs and broke her neck. Now she won't have to face that nasty little gallbladder operation. Aside from that it's been a great year.' And so forth."

Elinor laughed into the receiver. "You're quite right. Canadians do have a way of turning calamity into a sort of spiritual Jacuzzi. I don't think I'd be quite so effervescent if the apartment really was mine. It's in pretty bad shape. In the meantime I'll take the sheets I used over to Mother's. She has a washer and dryer. I'll press them and leave them with the doorman. There must be fresh sheets in one of the closets, so I can make up the bed."

"Better still, Elinor, why don't you just stay put?"

"That's very kind of you Geoffry, but I don't like to impose."

"You misunderstand me. What I propose is strictly business. Why don't you sublet Mother's apartment. The lease runs until May first. As I think I told you, I am keeping the place intact until Mother is certain she wants to remain at Maple Grove. However, my sister has her knickers in a twist because the place is standing empty and we are paying rent. No doubt it is an extravagance, but Mother is an old lady. Her wants are few, and this move, as we all tacitly acknowledge, will be her last. I want it to be user friendly. Were you to stay on at Mother's it would be with the understanding that she could decide to move back. The possibility is slight, but it is nonetheless there. But why move to a dreary little service flat when you could stay on comfortably where you are and earn me points with my sister at the same time."

"Goodness me, Geoffry, what a tempting offer, so tempting in fact that in my true-north fashion I feel I should say no. I mean, why take the easy way out when you can throw up needless obstacles?"

"Then it's settled. Now, you offered to brandish your credit card and take me out to lunch. How about today, say around one o'clock at my office. Then we can work out the details."

"I'll be there, Mastercard at the ready. You're quite sure you mean what you say? You're not going to yank the football away just as I kick, like the bossy little girl in the *Peanuts* comic strip?"

"That bossy little girl is my sister, not me. One o'clock then."

I replaced the receiver already anticipating the call I would make to my sister telling her that Mother's apartment was sublet and bringing in revenue. I knew Elinor would be a responsible tenant and that she shared the concept that property demands respect, even if it is not one's own.

It is a long time since I have met anyone, male or female, with Elinor's particular slant. She understood a party is for diversion, not an excuse to get some man off in a corner and fuck his mind. She was not on the make, and – God only knows – neither was I. But the older one gets the more difficult it becomes to make new friends. The defenses are so firmly in place they become nearly impossible to breach, from either side. As I reached for the letters I had to sign, I glanced at my watch realizing I was actually looking forward to lunch.

I wonder if social historians will one day trace the radical recession in the final decades of the Twentieth Century to the decline of the three-martini lunch. Back in the fifties, sixties, as late as the seventies, business executives routinely ordered martinis before lunch and returned stinko to their offices to make millions. Nowadays their junior counterparts drink white wine, imported mineral waters, and energizing concoctions involving vegetables and a blender. The economy has taken a nosedive. My premise may not yet have found its way into the textbooks, but it is no more implausible than many of the explanations routinely served up by business columnists in our national newspapers.

I too abandoned the three-martini lunch over a decade ago. Martinis make me frisky, and drinking them at noon caused me more than once to cancel my afternoon appointments and skip off to the bars. From then on until the small hours my behaviour was frankly irresponsible. It was also marvellous fun. That was the time when being in the company of other gay men had cachet. We were part of a secret fraternity, like the Masons, and every time we got it on we felt we were giving society the finger. Pleasure is more intense when seasoned with a little guilt, a little anxiety, or at the very least, the feeling of pulling a fast one. Nowadays homosexuals have become strident, political, and, above all, visible. Yesterday's closet case has become today's activist, tossing his curls, stamping his foot, and demanding conjugal rights, equal opportunity, increased government funding. The scene, as they say, has become impossibly dreary. Casual sex with a total stranger no longer signifies an act of rebellion but a major risk to your health. To pass judgement is out of fashion, like bubble hairdos, and with no more perpetrators there are only victims.

Too much tolerance is stultifying, particularly to one who can remember when sex with girls was considered naughty. With no more forbidden boundaries to cross we have turned back onto ourselves: shrinkwrapped magazines, pornographic videos, and telephone sex as quick alternatives to relationships sanctified by affection, sometimes by love. That formerly turgid emotion has been tamed into having someone special being there for you. Maybe monks have a point after all.

Elinor arrived at my office promptly at one. "I hope we don't run into anyone from last night's party," she whispered. "I'm wearing the same dress, and you know how people jump to conclusions."

"Little Orphan Annie always wore the same little red dress, and nobody suspected her."

"Yes, but she had that daunting dog to protect her virtue. Do you have a restaurant in mind?"

I suggested an Italian restaurant within walking distance. There are booths where one can talk privately, and the menu goes beyond pizza and pasta with tomato sauce. Elinor chose an excellent Chianti from the wine list. I occasionally drink wine at lunch, followed by a double espresso before I return to the office.

The business part of our meeting took only minutes. I explained again how Mother deciding to return to her apartment would negate our agreement. As a tradeoff, were Elinor to find a place she preferred she would be at liberty to move out whenever she wished. I inquired what rent she had been paying at her current apartment. She named a figure. I asked if she would be prepared to pay the same amount for Mother's flat. Yes, indeed, she replied; it was a far larger and more elegant apartment than the one she now had. Ought she to pay more? Not necessarily; Mother and I were still coming out ahead, as I had expected the place to stand empty until the lease expired. We shook hands on the deal and turned our attention to the menu.

"I was amused at your observation," she began, our order having been placed, "at how Canadians turn disaster into a hidden benefit. But, to tell the truth, I really quite dreaded Christmas." She took a sip of wine. "I'm not making a bid for sympathy, but this will be my first holiday season since Andrew died. Something about Christmas intensifies reactions. Jokes seem funnier, petty irritations turn into disasters, and minor fits of depression can drag you down for days. Your helping me find a safe haven will make the next few days easier to negotiate."

"I don't know how much Christmas spirit you can absorb," I said, but there is a small artificial tree in Mother's storage locker, along with some ornaments. Would you like me to set it up for you?"

"That would be delightful. If you'd like to drop by some evening on your way home from the office you could bring up the tree, and I'll give you some dinner."

"You don't have to do that."

"It would be my pleasure." She smiled, and for just a second something shimmered between us, a gleam of awareness, recognition, anticipation. I have long passed the age when I was a deb's delight, but I am single and I don't have two heads. Here I was, seated across the table from a vital and attractive woman recently widowed, who quite obviously liked me. Much as I dislike wearing a sandwich board, there are situations where an ounce of candour is worth a ton of cure.

"I would like that," I said, choosing my words carefully. "This Christmas promises to be bumpier than most for me as well. A close friend, my very close friend died only recently and – as you have suggested, Christmas throws everything into sharp relief."

Elinor did not skip a beat. "By friend, do you mean long-time companion?"

"Yes."

As if prompted, the waiter arrived with our Caesar salads. When he had moved out of earshot I picked up the thread.

"We hadn't been together that long, not quite six years, but we first met during the sixties. We came together and separated, like so many during those freewheeling years. Making love was our surrogate religion."

" 'Ah, yes, I remember it well.' You obviously ran into each other again."

"Quite by accident. I went for professional advice and discovered that Pat had turned into Patrick Fitzgerald Associates. By then he had divorced his wife. We became friends."

Elinor smiled. "I take it the first time around you were too busy to have time for friendship."

I repressed a laugh. "You might say. This time around the fires were banked, but we were hugely compatible. I have never known a person more comfortable to be with. We talked seriously about retirement. One morning he had a heart attack. And that was the end of that."

"And now you find each day has about forty-eight hours."

"That about says it."

We paused to eat before Elinor spoke. "I used to think of love as a heightened form of desire. Can you still remember desire, that longing for someone so intense that even having the person beside you in bed could barely assuage it?"

"Indeed I do remember. Lust is when your body has hot pants. Desire is more like a crotch fog of the spirit."

We both laughed into our plates. Elinor reached for her wine glass. "It's funny, but I guess at some point we all thought of love as passion at white heat. Now, with two children and one remarriage under my belt, I wonder if love isn't a tolerance for repetition: the same jokes, the same laundry, the same meat loaf on Friday nights, even the same lovemaking. I mean, the *Kama Sutra* may be all very well in a silk draped pavilion, but in suburban Toronto?"

"Or in Westmount for that matter. I've always thought the *Kama Sutra* was less about eroticism than agility. Doing the dirty deed while standing on one foot? Gimme a break!"

By now into our second glass of wine, we shared a comfortable chuckle.

"Geoffry, I hope you don't mind my asking, but I did see your wedding picture last night, on your mother's dresser."

"Yes, you did. As I told you, my wife and infant daughter died in a traffic accident early in the marriage. I mourned, but youth is resilient. As my life began to pick up momentum once again I came to realize there were tempting alternatives to the strict values on which I had been raised. I went down the road not taken. I think you can fill in the blanks."

"Easily. I have always been very partial to men, so much so in fact, I find it odd that everyone isn't partial to them."

Our veal arrived and we began to eat.

"Do you have someone to help you move your things?"

"My son Gregory will give me a hand. A fire imposes its own imperatives. My daughter has excused me from sitting with her children this evening so Greg can help me move. When would you like to come by and set up the tree?"

"Tomorrow or Wednesday. Thursday is Christmas Eve."

"How about tomorrow. I'm not a fussy cook, so we can eat anytime you like. I would suggest bringing up the tree before we eat, while you are still lean and hungry. Then we can hang the ornaments while we have a pre-prandial drink. Andrew liked a few pops before he ate, so I never cooked anything that couldn't be kept warm. Did you know I was crowned Casserole Queen of 1987? Is there anything you can't or shouldn't eat?"

"I have no food allergies and my cholesterol count is normal. I like beef well cooked, not throbbing on the plate, and I draw the line at tunafish casserole."

Elinor giggled into her napkin. "I had a couple of gay friends at college. I used to go by their tiny student apartment for dinner and eat tunafish casserole, or 'fruit pie,' as they called it."

"Precisely. It was the native food of our generation. Take a tin of cream of mushroom soup, one package of noodles, and two tins of tuna."

"With chopped red pepper for colour interest – and don't forget the Velveeta!"

"Without being fulsome, Elinor, I didn't think you were old enough to remember tunafish casserole."

"Thank you, kind sir, but, alas, I am. I can also remember that you are a working lawyer. Shouldn't you be getting back to your office?

"I suppose you're right."

"If you can get our waiter's attention I'll settle the bill while we have coffee. I'm going to need something to help me pack all those smoky clothes into bags."

I signalled to the maitre d'; that way the cheque arrives promptly.

Tuesday afternoon I swung by my apartment before heading over to Mother's building for dinner with Elinor. Nodding a guarded greeting to the doorman, I collected my mail from the box in an alcove in the lobby and rode the elevator to my floor. It took only a minute to change into gray slacks, a blue button-down shirt, and navy blue crew necked sweater – the uniform of the ageing preppie. As I had plenty of time I poured myself a Scotch and sat down at the kitchen table to go through the mail. Some envelopes I didn't bother to open, such as the one featuring a grubby waif in Dickensian rags who apparently was going to go hungry on Christmas Day unless I wrote a cheque. Much as I dislike the pornography of poverty, I could be tempted to send money if I could believe for ten seconds that a hungry child might benefit and not some incompetent bureaucrat skimming a salary and perks off the top. Nor did I want an endless series of gardening books. In a world gone mad for horticulture I do not even have flower boxes on my terrace. Bills could be dealt with at my office. There remained the Christmas cards which still arrive from those staunch souls who refuse to be deflected by my never sending a card in return. The first one I opened was from my sister Mildred. Now that her children are grown up and dispersed they no longer end up on her Christmas cards. Instead she uses an artistic photograph she has snapped herself, photography being one of the worthy pursuits she has taken up since her husband died. This year the image was of a covered bridge seen across a field of daisies, a considerable improvement over last year's Labrador puppies.

A couple of cards came from former lady friends, less, I suspect, to insist I have the happiest Christmas possible than to remind themselves there had been a life before children, upwardly mobile husbands, singing in *Messiah* to raise money for repairing the church roof, and coffee parties for local federal candidates. I reached for an envelope which bore no return address and slit it open with a kitchen knife. Patrick used to say that using a paring knife to open mail blunted the edge. I in turn would suggest that knives can be sharpened or replaced. It was one of those exchanges people who live together frequently have: banal, pointless, and infinitely reassuring. I slid out one of those cards that gives Christmas a bad name. A jolly Santa, whose corpulence and high colour suggested a heart attack lurking behind the next chimney, was playing baseball with the reindeer. (I suppose eight reindeer plus Rudolph makes a team.) Inside the message read: "Hit that ball / And don't forget / To have the merriest Christmas yet!" Underneath had been typed: "Your Christmas is not going to be very merry, believe me. In fact, it may well be your last."

I would like to think of myself as a prudent man, not a violent one, but instead of feeling apprehension I was flooded with rage. Fantasies of inflicting real pain on my unknown and unpleasant adversary pushed aside thoughts of taking precautions. I am not certain why I felt this way, unless perhaps because a physical threat is an extreme violation of privacy, and privacy, mine or anyone else's, is one of the few defenses we can retain against an increasingly overcrowded and voraciously inquisitive world. Forgetting the rest of my mail, I finished my drink in one swallow and left the apartment, so abruptly, in fact, that I was at the door of Mother's building when I realized I had left behind the bottle of wine I had intended to bring as a threshold present.

Elinor opened the door to the apartment wearing a full-skirted blue cotton dress. As I came down the hallway, she dropped a curtsey.

"I feel a bit foolish in a summer frock, but all my adult clothes are at the cleaners because of the fire. So you will just have to accept me as the farmer's daughter."

I pantomimed twirling my moustache. "Be not so arch, proud beauty. If you don't have the rent money I'll send you shivering into the night – and your little dog too."

"Oh please, kind sir, could we not negotiate, say over a double Scotch on the rocks?"

"Curses! Foiled again!" I hung up my coat. "The bottle of wine I intended to bring is sitting on my kitchen counter, but it's the thought that counts. Now, while you pour drinks I'll go down and fetch the tree."

"Do you need a hand?" inquired Elinor. "I could carry the ornaments."

"That would be agreeable. Then I won't have to make two trips."

Leaving the apartment door slightly ajar, we rode down to street level. Beside the elevator a flight of stairs led down to the kind of basement that could make anyone feel apprehensive. Rows of storage lockers with wire mesh doors, knocked together from rough slats, reminded me of holding cells for prisoners in one of those movies which gleefully exploits man's inhumanity to man.

Wrapped in a sheet, the small tree rested against a pyramid of suitcases. Elinor carried the ornaments, packed like eggs in soft cardboard boxes, while I took the tree and a bag of lights. I locked the door and we retraced our steps to the elevator, then up to the top floor. To our surprise the apartment door was shut.

"That's odd," said Elinor. "I left nothing open, so it can't have been a draft."

"Luckily I have a key on my ring." About to unlock the door I heard voices. "There's someone inside." Instead I gave the buzzer three sharp rings.

The door flew open. "Geoffry! I wondered where you'd got to. The doorman told me you were upstairs."

"Mildred! What on earth are you doing here?"

"I've come to spend Christmas with Mother. With the apartment standing empty, I thought it a golden opportunity." Suddenly aware that I was not alone, Mildred acknowledged Elinor with a look. "How do you do. I'm Mildred Carson, Geoffry's sister."

"Elinor Richardson. Excuse my not shaking hands, but I'd hate to drop the ornaments."

"Oh, good," said Mildred, "I see you've brought up the tree. Mother will be so pleased. I'm going to cook Christmas dinner and she plans to come. It will be her last Christmas in the flat. I telephoned her from Toronto. Don't just stand there. Come inside."

As she turned to lead the way, I looked at Elinor and shrugged. Realizing I had been caught off guard, she gave me a smile and followed me inside.

"Is that Uncle Geoffry?" inquired a voice, and my niece came into the living room where we all stood awkwardly. Jennifer was obviously Mildred's daughter, but luminous with the bloom of youth.

"My niece Jennifer, Elinor Richardson." I said, still holding the tree like a major domo's staff. Elinor put down the boxes and shook hands, whereupon Jennifer approached to kiss me on both cheeks.

"I went to collect Mother at Central Station."

"So I see." I laid the tree on the hearth. "Mildred, we have a small problem. Correction: we have had a stroke of luck. Elinor has sublet Mother's apartment, either until the lease expires or until Mother decides to move back, should she decide to do so."

My sister does not like surprises. "When did this happen?" she demanded. "And why didn't you telephone to inform me?"

"I was going to, this evening in fact. It all happened rather suddenly. Elinor was burned out of her apartment on Sunday night and needed a place to stay. I knew you were concerned about the apartment standing empty, so I came up with what I thought to be a logical solution."

I could see Mildred trying without much success to battle outrage. She had arrived to spend Christmas at Mother's apartment, only to find herself dispossessed. Her face assumed the expression of someone who has just been goosed on the elevator.

"I think you might at least have consulted me."

"Why don't we all sit down?" suggested Jennifer diplomatically. We sat stiffly, as if given the nod by royalty.

Elinor spoke, "Jennifer, do you live in Montreal?"

"Yes, I have a studio apartment. I also have a foam mattress and a duvet. Mother can use the bed."

"That sounds a bit Third World for the Christmas holiday," suggested Elinor. "Mildred, how long do you plan to stay?"

"I have a return reservation for Sunday morning, the day after Boxing Day."

"In that case," said Elinor leaning forward, "I have a sug-

gestion. If you don't mind sleeping in your mother's room, why
don't you stay here? There are two bathrooms, and I can give
you a hand with Christmas dinner."

Mildred raised her eyebrows and her chin; Jennifer smiled;
I spoke. "That's very generous of you, Elinor, but not necessary.
You are now the official tenant, and you must not feel obligated."

"I don't. But sleeping on the floor is not festive. And
money spent on a hotel does seem extravagant when a perfectly
good bedroom is waiting to be used."

Mildred bestirred herself to say something civil. "That is
very kind of you, Elinor. If you're sure you don't mind." If there
was grace in her tone there was none in her rigid and unsmiling
demeanour.

Elinor stood. "Geoffry, I promised you a drink. And I have
food on the stove. It can easily be stretched to serve everyone."

"That sounds fine," said Mildred. "So does a drink."

Now Jennifer stood. "Thank you, Elinor, but Mother and I
are going out. We haven't seen each other for a while. Mother,
you can unpack later." She gave her mother the laser look, and
the two women filed out.

Elinor poured drinks while I set up the tree in front of the
window. "I hope you won't regret your invitation," I began after
we touched glasses and drank. "Mildred is not the easiest
woman to bunk in with. I draw daily comfort from the fact that
she is not twins."

"It's only until Sunday morning. And with all the Christmas coming and going she'll get lost in the shuffle. By the way,
do you mind if I have a few people in on Christmas Eve? I had
already invited them to the other apartment, but I can easily
put them off."

"Do nothing of the sort. Remember, this is now your home."

Elinor began to open boxes of blown-glass ornaments. "If you have nothing better to do on Christmas Eve, please come. I'll set up a bar and make a large platter of sandwiches. My son Gregory will probably drop by. And Mother tells me my cousin by marriage is coming to Montreal for Christmas. He is recently divorced and perhaps at loose ends. I suppose I should invite him too, although he may have other plans. I've asked my good friend, Amy, Amy Hutchins. It turns out her son isn't coming in for Christmas after all, so she's on her own. It will be a casual evening, people drifting in and out. Not a mob."

"Amy Hutchins," I repeated, "a small brunette with enormous dark eyes in a triangular face?"

"That's Amy. How do you know her?"

"We met some years ago, but only briefly."

I did not elaborate. My encounter with Amy had been one of those tasteless episodes I would rather forget. Amy had been having an affair with Hartland Crawford who, in order to square his absences with Audrey, used me as an alibi. What got my back up was that he failed to clear the whole thing with me first, but telephoned my office to explain he found himself in a bit of a jam. Audrey had dropped by his office one afternoon without warning only to find him gone. When questioned, Hartland lied glibly and said he had been playing tennis with Geoffry Chadwick. Would I mind awfully backing up his story?

To tell the truth, I did mind awfully. I have always considered Hartland an asshole, more precisely the tedious kind of straight male who behaves like a child when dealing with his own appetites. For Hartland instant gratification is far too slow. Over the years he has indulged in his share of sleeping around, or having sex, depending on the decade. A man who wears a gray flannel suit like a uniform, he mistakenly believes no one will recognize him if he wears a windbreaker and a baseball cap to an assignation.

I suspect Audrey has looked at her share of ceilings, but she understands the value of discretion. Although there have been times when I have wanted to push her, fully dressed, into the deep end of the nearest swimming pool, I did not want to see my friend embarrassed by her husband's sleazy little affair. So I told the social lie and admitted to playing tennis with Hartland.

"But I thought you detested sports and games," Audrey had said.

"I do, but my doctor insists on my getting more exercise."

The conversation shifted into other channels, and I considered the episode filed away, until one evening I walked into the Ritz Bar to see Hartland having a drink with a woman definitely not his wife. In fact she was everything Audrey is not: small, dark, gamine, with large, soft eyes – the kind that make some people think of a doe, others of a cocker spaniel. I couldn't imagine a more public place for a tryst than the Ritz Bar, except possibly on camera at one of the local television stations, but Hartland has never been sicklied o'er with the pale cast of thought.

I was summoned to join them. "Geoffry Chadwick, meet Amy Hutchins." We shook hands. "Geoffry is the one who covered my ass." Before I could mouth excuses, Hartland nailed a waiter and ordered a double Black Label on the rocks. Who am I to look a gift Scotch in the tumbler? And I admitted to some curiosity about the other woman.

The other woman wasted no time crossing her legs in my

direction and tuning out Hartland as though he were the bus boy. When my drink arrived she asked if she could have a sip; she didn't know what Black Label tasted like.

"It tastes just like Scotch," I replied. As I handed her the glass I thought that were I on the bench I would speedily acquit axe murderers who did in women who said, "I won't have a drink; I'll just have a sip of his."

Amy then began to question me about my domestic arrangements. As always I was deliberately vague, until Hartland blurted out that my wife had been killed and that I lived alone.

Amy leaned a little bit closer and asked what I did for excitement. I replied that my doctor had absolutely forbidden excitement of any kind, and as for living alone, well, I had my pacemaker, my artificial knee, and my catheter for company. As I did not crack a smile, Amy found herself checked. "I've also had a charisma bypass and I'm at brain death's door." I added, letting her know she had been sent up.

"Oh, well, " she retorted, "at least your tits aren't full of silicone and your ass of PolyFilla."

We both laughed the laughter of a declared truce. Hartland, who had been watching from the sidelines, looked purposefully at his watch and announced it was time to go. He paid the bill and they left, leaving me to finish my drink in peace.

When I next ran into Hartland some weeks later, I inquired after Amy. He made noises in the back of his throat and looked at the sidewalk. I was able to unscramble a few phrases: "only out for herself, not one of us, whatever was I thinking of." I surmised the affair had ended.

But I had the last word. "Hartland, for Audrey's sake I covered your tracks. I won't do it again." Without waiting for a reply I went on my way.

I did not think it necessary to relay any of this to Elinor, so I merely observed, "Sounds good. I don't really enjoy crowd scenes. And speaking of good, that drink went down pretty quickly. My sister has that effect on me. Do you suppose there's more where that came from?"

"As much as you like. Let me know when you would like to eat. I can have dinner on the table in five minutes. Perhaps you'd better string the lights on the tree before I hang ornaments. It cuts down on breakage."

Trimming the small tree did not take long, and soon we were comfortably settled with our drinks. Rather than take the wingbacked chair to the right of the fireplace, I chose a small chair to the left. "I can't help thinking of that as Mother's chair. It's where she always sat. I suggested she take it with her to Maple Grove, but she wanted to remember the room the way it was."

"I can understand that. It's a lovely apartment. She must have been reluctant to leave it." Elinor paused to drink. "Does Mildred have other children besides Jennifer?"

"Two. A son who is a musician. He plays the harpsichord, for reasons which are clear to him. At the moment he is on a concert tour in the U.K. There is a second daughter who is supposed to be studying voice. She's not completely without talent, but close. I understand she is spending Christmas with her current boyfriend. The turnover is high. Jennifer is the youngest and the pick of the litter. At the moment she is teaching at a private school."

"Does she have a beau? She certainly is pretty."

"She is, but I don't think so. She was engaged for a while,

but the young man turned out to be sexually ambivalent, to put it kindly. Happily she found out before the wedding. Did I understand you to say you were a grandmother? You must have been a child bride."

"In a manner of speaking. I married when I graduated from university and had my children in short order. Then I divorced, and managed to snatch defeat from the jaws of compromise. My daughter Jane has two small children and is working away at a law degree between loads of laundry. Now that I'm in Montreal, I can help out when she is stuck, but I am the first to admit I am a delinquent grandmother. I love my grand-children and all that Hallmark card party line, but a little goes a long way. I brought up two children of my own, and I've turned in my badge. Being a grandmother was easier before the advent of the cellular phone; now you are always on call. Would you like another Scotch before you eat?"

"Yes, please."

Elinor poured me a refill, then made a quick detour into the kitchen before sitting down. "My son, Gregory," she continued, "is an engineer and managed to land himself a good job here after graduation. Even though we lived in Toronto I made certain my kids learned to speak French. In his case it has paid off. He's tall and impossibly good looking. Jane calls him 'the album cover'."

We shared a quiet laugh, then Elinor suggested we might eat. Her Boeuf Bourguignon, that which we grandly called beef stew with red wine in the fifties, was excellent. We ate in the kitchen, which proved far more congenial for two than the formal dining room, and lingered over salad followed by a chunk of perfectly aged Stilton.

Over dinner Elinor talked about Amy. The subject of her
friend came up spontaneously. According to Elinor, men have
drifted in and out of Amy's life, never staying more than a few
weeks, until finally she found herself in a long term relationship. The man turned out to be an alcoholic whose marriage
was on the rocks. Amy, who calls herself an actress, meaning
she is unemployed, saw the affair as theatre. She was cast as the
woman in white, sympathetic and nurturing, an oasis of woman-
hood in a desert of strident feminism. She played the part well,
almost too well. Her best scenes happened when he fell off the
wagon with a resounding crash and took off on a three-day tear.
Almost prostrate with remorse, not to mention hangover, he
would slink back to her understanding, forgiving arms. Instead
of a harridan screaming recriminations, he found a wellspring
of womanly warmth, cradling his shaggy head on her comforting breast under a rose filtered spot coming from the left
about a foot above eye level.

After a while he stopped going off on benders and settled
down to a life of hard-working sobriety. Without the drama of
his drinking, Amy came to realize he was dreadfully dull. Com-
pounding the problem was that Amy herself likes a Scotch or
two in the evening before her dinner. No longer could she
drink when he was around; furthermore, he wanted his supper
at six, as soon as he got home from work. Always nocturnal,
Amy began to dread that endless stretch of time between
loading supper dishes into the dishwasher and sleep. Fearful of
breaking off the relationship lest he begin drinking and mess
up his life again, she marked time and longed for the final
curtain. When he was offered a good job in Halifax, from
whence he had come, Amy urged him to accept. At first he was

reluctant, but she stood firm. They parted friends.

Now she can drink Scotch and eat whenever she likes, only she does so alone. Although reluctant to admit the fact, even to herself, Amy has reached the age when she would like a permanent relationship, with the consequent tradeoff of electricity for stability. Romance is exhausting, and we come to a point when a night of pure amour with little sleep leaves us bleary eyed and groggy the next day, something I discovered some years ago.

I found myself enjoying Elinor's company, not surprisingly as I have always sought out the society of women. Many men who boast of their success with women in bed do not really like them fully dressed and standing upright. Otherwise why would they choose to hang out with the guys. One of life's drearier scenarios involves a group of men, all of whom are wearing plastic mesh baseball caps and nylon windbreakers, backed up by a few cases of beer and a football. They bond to beat the band and bore themselves to death in the process, their idea of a good time limiting itself to being in the company of other men without women present. As a boy I can remember being taunted and called a sissy for playing with girls. When I beat the shit out of my tormentor I was accused of fighting dirty. Always prepared to believe we inhabit an unjust world, I also believe there are no baseball caps in heaven.

"Do you enjoy being back in Montreal?" I asked over herbal tea, yet another capitulation to the passage of time.

"Yes, I do. I grew up here, remember, but the city has changed. The simple division of English-French has become clouded by waves of immigration. Nowadays it's possible to experience culture shock without leaving the block."

I smiled. "I guess you're right." Gripping the sides of the

table with both hands I struck an attitude. "Now, when I was a boy . . . my father, bless his heart, used to begin stories like that. When he was a boy the world was a better place. Men were manlier, women more womanly, the air was fresher, and everybody pulled his weight. I don't know whether things were better when we were younger, but at least strangers didn't ask about your zodiac sign, or whether you believed in reincarnation."

Elinor laughed her easy, infectious laugh. "True enough. 'What is your sign?' has replaced 'Haven't I seen you somewhere before?' as the standard pickup line. I don't happen to believe in reincarnation, but I'm hedging my bets. Should I come back it will be as a Teddy bear: everybody loves you; nobody cares if you're fat; and you grow more valuable with age."

Our conversation was interrupted by the sound of the front door closing. Still wearing her mink, Mildred strode into the kitchen.

"You're still here, Geoffry."

"Obviously."

"Good evening, Mildred," said Elinor.

"Elinor."

Rising to my feet, the better to do battle, I spoke. "Mildred, I didn't want to get into this earlier, but what is this madcap scheme of dragging Mother back here for Christmas dinner? She's settling in nicely at Maple Grove Manor; I was to join her for Christmas dinner there. And now you want to get her all stirred up and nostalgic for home."

"Don't be ridiculous, Geoffry. She'll enjoy the change."

"Mother dislikes change even more than I do. What happens when she has a few vodkas and becomes . . . tired and emotional? And with other people around she'll be worse."

"She doesn't have to drink."

"Oh yes she does, and as much as she wants. We are not going to celebrate Christmas by tossing her onto the wagon. My advice is for you to visit her tomorrow and persuade her to stay put. We can both have our Christmas dinner at Maple Grove. Turkey is turkey, dry and dull no matter where you eat it."

"I'll do no such thing. She would be dreadfully disappointed if I reneged on my invitation. And Elinor has agreed to help. Didn't you, Elinor?"

I honestly believe Vlad the Impaler would have replied yes to that unequivocal demand. Elinor certainly did.

"Very well, dear sister, be it on your head. But if Mother does decide to move back home because of the Xmas festivities you had better be prepared to move down and take care of her, at least until we find someone qualified and trustworthy. Boys don't help their mothers in and out of the bathtub."

"Oh, Geoffry, you always make such a fuss. I'm going to unpack." Mildred went off to hang up her coat and returned to stand in the kitchen door. "Elinor, if you don't mind, there's a small television set in the maid's room, the one you're using. I'd like to take it into Mother's room. I like to fall asleep watching TV."

"So do I," said Elinor, as if answering a request for the time. "There's a large TV console in the den which will give you a much better picture than the poky little set in my room. And now while you unpack I must tidy up the kitchen."

Mildred is not a good loser. She stalked from the kitchen without saying goodnight. I could have applauded. Elinor was not about to let herself be bullied by Mildred. As I said thanks and goodnight, I felt much better about my sister's sudden visit.

Mother used to say about overbearing people that if you give them an inch they'll take a mile. In Mildred's case if you give her an inch she'll take a square mile, but Elinor was not about to forfeit that initial inch.

IV

The night was clear but not cold, and, as I did not have far to go, I set off on foot. A short walk was welcome for several reasons. The first was a chance to simmer down after my near confrontation with Mildred. I did not think bringing Mother back to her apartment for a slice of overcooked turkey served with cranberry and confusion was a good idea. Christmas is awash in fake emotion, and I feared Mother would begin to wax nostalgic for the good old days, especially after a few vodkas. Even sober, Mother tends to airbrush the past, and there was more than a little chance that the combination of liquor and memories would convince her that happiness lay in familiarity.

Had Mildred not already broached the idea to Mother, I would have pulled rank and forbidden it, but I dislike family confrontations, especially in front of other people. I did not want to subject Elinor to an internecine Chadwick squabble. As it stands, the poor woman has scant idea of what she has let herself in for. She will have her hands full just keeping her guard up; otherwise she will be treated like a charity case even though she is paying the rent.

My second reason for deciding to walk was that I was not in the least hurry to learn if any further messages had been left with my answering service. There are situations one wishes would simply go away, and this was definitely one of those.

Further harassment must oblige me to take some sort of action, and I dreaded the thought of approaching some burly and indifferent police officer with an "Er-um, excuse me, but I have been receiving some threatening calls and messages." I would feel foolish, and I share the universal dislike of appearing ridiculous, more so in front of those I do not consider my equals. I would be drawing attention to myself, something I was raised to believe was a dreadful social gaffe – in the same way that illness was considered bad form. Get yourself to the emergency ward if you must, but try not to disturb anybody. Never laugh too loud, or raise your voice, or succumb to anger, that most seductive of unruly emotions. To be bothered by telephone calls should remain a personal annoyance and, like a hangover or a skin rash, ought to be dealt with in private.

My final reason for deciding to walk had to do with delaying the inevitable, namely turning the key and letting myself into an empty apartment. Only last year a three bedroom apartment had become available in my building. I signed the lease and Patrick moved in with me, taking the two extra bedrooms for his own use.

The arrangement worked well, and this coming spring we had intended to look for a house in the country, a place that would be truly ours. Then he died. I suppose I should move; I don't need three bedrooms. But to relinquish the apartment would mean letting go, and I am not quite ready for that.

Years ago my mother fell and broke her wrist. Far from lamenting the inconvenience, she felt the plaster cast bestowed importance, like medals or a diploma; she delighted in showing it off. My father suggested it was a rare instance of pride coming after a fall. There was a time when I prided myself on my self-sufficiency. People spun in and out of my life, drawn by love or desire, and whirled away just as rapidly once the intense, evanescent flame had burned itself out. Somehow I knew, even back then, that when you say "I love you" to somebody, you have started to say goodbye.

I can't remember ever telling Patrick that I loved him. But I did, and he knew it. Having once fallen in lust, the second time around we found companionship and congeniality. That is what I miss, more than I care to admit. Coming home together after an evening out, we would share a quiet beer and discuss what we had done, whom we had seen. Being a night person, he was still puttering about when I fell asleep. Often I left for the office before he awoke. But he had been there, just there, a warm, breathing presence. His death revealed gaping holes in my armour of self-sufficiency, forcing me to realize I am human just like everyone else. The discovery did not fill me with delight.

Elinor must be going through a similar period of adjustment, but I derive no comfort from the thought. Misery is said to like company, but knowing that other people are wet and shivering does not make me feel warm and dry. I hope we can be friends. She does not strike me as a woman who has to be in control. Too many women treat gay men with a kind of affable condescension, almost as if they were rejected suitors.

I seriously doubt that Elinor would find a way to tell me I drink too much and don't eat properly. She would not offer to stock my refrigerator with delicacies from her freezer, nor suggest rearranging the living room furniture. She would not offer to rehang my pictures. I can't imagine she would presume to buy me ties, putty-coloured repp hinting my taste is too flamboyant, or psychedelic Italian silks suggesting that my life lacks colour.

For my part I would not ask whether she has ever considered tinting her hair, say ash blond. When she has taken the trouble to dress for an evening in earth tones I wouldn't tell her she would look fabulous in pink. I would not oblige her to sit through the mad scene from *Lucia di Lamermoor* sung by five different sopranos, expatiating at length on the merits of each. I would not spend the evening talking about old movies and how gays have been given a bum rap by Hollywood. I would not present myself as a victim. And I would never round off a pleasant and civil evening by taking her to a gay bar. Finally, I would help her on and off with her coat, hold the car door, and push in her chair, unless she requested me not to, although I seriously doubt she would.

To my relief there were no messages on my machine. Even so, I popped a couple of aspirins to help me sleep. Since Patrick died, I wake even earlier than I used to, and the next morning, Wednesday, was no exception. As the week prior to Christmas is seldom busy, I decided to stop in at the health club on my way to the office.

Christmas inertia appeared to have struck down the exercise business, and the locker room stood empty. I changed quickly and went directly to the cardiovascular room: treadmill, Stairmaster, bicycle. I suppose I should use those fifteen-minute stretches of mindless exercise to sort out work-related problems, but the monotonous physical rhythm tends to numb the thought process. My mind seems to empty itself, to the point where if someone asked my name I would have to pause briefly before answering.

It took me a couple of blanked-out seconds to realize that the woman who had just walked into the room was Elinor. Her "Good morning, Geoffry," roused me from my quasi-coma. I wouldn't say Elinor looked good in workout clothes; few women do, but she wore them easily. She did not make a fashion statement, nor did she look like a bag lady. I blotted my face with the towel slung around my neck and smiled. "Are you working off last night's dinner?" she asked.

"Is that a trick question?"

"Not completely. I'm here to do penance for the entire holiday season."

"How now, Elinor, surely you're not feeling guilt. The year I turned forty I realized guilt belongs on eighteenth-century furniture. Besides, all things are possible during our great Christian festival."

"When I turned thirty I realized guilt was ecumenical, from Mount Olympus to Mount Sinai to Mount Royal. I think that was the year my children solemnly informed me there was no Santa Claus. They had already banished the Easter Bunny and the Tooth Fairy, so I knew Santa was living on borrowed time. I took them into my confidence, in the profoundly dishonest way of parents who put their well-being before that of their children, and convinced them that without Santa Claus Christmas Day was just another birthday party and therefore, to be celebrated with considerably less fuss.

"It was probably the children's first real experience with the downside of truth. Puffed up and humourless with their newfound knowledge, they still wanted all the trappings of Christmas. They hung stockings from the mantlepiece which I, in an act of denial for which I will pay dearly in the afterlife, refused to fill. "How can a Santa who doesn't exist fill your stockings?" I asked with the guile that masquerades as logic. Needless to say Christmas that year was a near disaster, with tears just below the surface, and a double helping of guilt. I guess it serves me right for trying to debunk one of the more durable myths."

I found myself laughing out loud. "That's a wonderful story. By the way, how are you managing with my kid sister?"

"All right, I guess."

"Good, but hang tough. Like most people, Mildred will push. Just hold your ground. I'm off for ten minutes in the weight room; then I must get back to the office."

"Will I see you tomorrow evening? I promise you on my Guide's honour we won't sing carols."

"Wouldn't miss it for the world. What time?"

"Anytime after six."

I nodded and left, hurrying back to the office only to be alarmed by a message that a Mr. Lawrence Townsend had telephoned. He was in town and wanted me to return the call. Try as we may, we never shake ourselves free from the past, and Lawrence Townsend II is a part of mine, a part which except for him I have left behind.

We have known one another since high school. He was one of the first adolescent males with whom I fooled around, which established us both as members of the secret fraternity. Since then Larry has lived his life as a kind of sexual double agent, or so he likes to think. He ignores, or refuses to admit the gay population has become visible, and still behaves as though he were hoodwinking the establishment. A highly successful real-estate agent, he appears as bland as butter to his prospective clients. Of medium height, trim, conservatively dressed, he blends into the crowd the way certain animals disappear into the surrounding foliage.

Once the business day ends he goes home to drink dry gin martinis. The effect of the cocktails is not dissimilar to that undergone by Dr. Jekyll when he drinks the potion. From sober businessman Larry turns into an outrageous, campy homosexual right before your eyes. Here the analogy breaks down. Mr. Hyde is the distillation of evil, whereas the drunken Larry grows merely tedious. He still refers to his male friends by the feminine pronoun: "Well, get her! she's not a well woman!" – a gay schtick that seemed amusing in the fifties. He relates his sexual adventures in exhaustive detail, and in doing so reveals the chase to be far more important than the capture. Once he has shed the mask of conciliatory salesman his emotional barometer fluctuates wildly. In seconds the most trivial discussion can erupt into a full-scale confrontation, often to the dismay of nearby patrons if we happen to be dining out. He may not be able to drink me under the proverbial table, but an evening on the town with him can lead to a hangover of mythic proportions. Larry is like dry vermouth in a martini or fresh garlic in a salad; a little goes a long way.

I suppose he is one of my oldest friends, but even that feel-good epithet hinges on what you expect an old friend to be. Anyone as potentially self-destructive as Larry will never be that fabled tower of strength, and any time spent drinking with him is a time of trouble. He would knock me flat and trample my prone body were I to be careless enough to stand between him and a trick. I long ago stopped taking him to restaurants I frequent, as I never know when he will embarrass me by groping the busboy or trying to date the waiter. I have lost track of the times I have put him to bed after he passed out, or lent him money because a trick stole his wallet, or tipped my way generously out of a restaurant after Larry had made his presence felt.

Why do I continue to see him? I wish I knew. It is not easy to exclude someone from your life, especially someone you have known for fifty years. Sometimes I wish I could muster that kind of ruthlessness, but I can't, even less so now that people I have known since school days are turning up with dismal regularity in the obituary column. I knew I couldn't avoid seeing Larry, but I could establish some ground rules. Christmas was a scant three days away, and I did not intend to embark upon the holiday season with a crippling hangover headache.

Thus resolved, I reached for the telephone and dialled the number Larry had left. He had obviously been expecting my call.

"Glinda the Good Witch of the North here," he said as he picked up the receiver. "Would you like me to snow on your poppies?"

"I am Oz, the Great and Powerful. And my balloon is leaving shortly. You called?"

"I want to put on the ruby slippers so that I can take you out to dinner."

"How long are you in Montreal?"

"Just for tonight. Yesterday I decided I wanted to spend Christmas in the sun – 'I'm dreaming of a green Christmas' – and the only flight my agent could find was out of Montreal."

"Dinner is fine," I said briskly, "with one proviso, that it be a sensible evening. The festive season is upon us, and I do not want to wake up tomorrow in a hospital ward with a needle in my arm."

"Lawsey, Miss Scarlett, when did you get dat old time religion?"

"I had an experience, like St. Paul on the road to Damascus, only mine happened in an aisle in the supermarket. I heard a voice say: 'Mend thy ways and fall no more into drunkenness. And today the frozen Shrimp Alfredo is on special.' The upshot is that I will go out for dinner but not an all-night drunk."

"Suits me. I have an early flight tomorrow."

"Good. Come to my apartment for a small drink first, say around seven." Even as I hung up I was trying to think of a restaurant with acceptable food where I was unlikely to return for at least a year.

Larry is generally prompt, and, true to form, at five minutes to seven the doorman rang to say I had a visitor. I found myself hoping Larry would have the elevator to himself. He was on vacation, meaning he probably had given himself a head start on the drinking hour. I fully expected him to burst out of the elevator shrieking a line from the movies. "I'm ready for my close-up, Mr. De Mille." Or, "I'd love to kiss you, but I just washed my hair."

Instead he walked quickly down the hall. "Dr. Chadwick, I presume?"

"Nightingale's the name – Florence. Here let me hang up your coat."

He looked around. "But you haven't decked the halls with boughs of holly. There's not even a sprig of mistletoe so you can kiss my bee-stung lips."

"I'm saving up for my big Easter display: a giant chocolate bunny surrounded by pots of Easter lilies, live baby chicks in the bathtub, an Easter egg hunt in the local library, and much,

much more. What will you drink? A mart?"

"Do you happen to have a beer?"

"A beer?"

"You heard me the first time. And it will be my first today. I'm having my period."

"Girls your age don't have periods. They have osteoporosis. I'll pour for the first hour."

"Stay as sweet as you are!" he called after me as I went into the kitchen.

We were soon facing each other across a low Queen Anne table. From where I sat I could see the Breuer chair Patrick had brought with him when he moved in. At one point in my life I would have fretted over its failure to blend in with my more traditional furnishings, its flagrant violation of the eleventh gay commandment: Thou shalt furnish thy room in good taste. It took me some years to realize that many with excellent taste in their surroundings show deplorable taste when it comes to conduct.

As a gesture to Larry's drinking beer, I had made my Scotch and water weaker than usual. "Why this sudden desire to head south? The whole world travels at Christmas, and February is a better month to get away."

"True. But suddenly I realized the holiday season beckoned and I had nothing to do. Oh, there were the usual parties, the same old faggot faces doing their stale routines. We've all had it on with one another over the years and about the only thing we have in common is that we are still alive."

"Lawrence my lad, you don't sound like yourself, as Mother would say. Are you sure you won't slide gently into a martini? You're sounding awfully glum."

"I'm not a well woman. But I wanted you to see me sober, to demonstrate that it can happen. Besides, I have something to discuss, a business proposition of sorts, and I never drink on the job."

"I'm all ears."

Larry put down his glass and leaned forward. "Geoffry, we've known each other a long time, right?"

"Longer than I'd care to admit."

"And we've been through the mill, right?"

"Through the mill, to the cleaners, and around the track."

"Good. Then why beat around the bush. What would you say to my moving down to Montreal so we could live together? Wait! Before you fling open the window and jump, hear me out. I'm not suggesting for a second we be anything but room-mates. We could never be lovers. We're sisters. But you're on your own, now that Patrick is – gone."

"Dead."

"Okay, dead. I'm awfully tired of living alone. Maybe you are too. And nobody knows me better than you do. On the household side, we'd split expenses right down the middle."

As the full implications of what Larry was suggesting took shape I was swept with a feeling very close to panic. That I would even consider living with him was out of the question. I truly would fling open the window and jump.

"Larry, you have lived in Toronto most of your adult life. All your friends are there. What about your business?"

"I don't have many friends, damn few if the truth were told. Mostly former tricks, business associates, and those, who in spite of easy affability, are scarcely more than acquaintances. As for business, real estate has picked up again across the board.

Our company has a Montreal office. Houses are houses. And one of these days I plan to retire."

The prospect of Larry sitting around the apartment all day would strike alarm into a stouter heart than mine.

"I don't know, Larry," I temporized, "I'm pretty set in my ways. You can't teach an old dog new tricks. And speaking of tricks, I don't fancy beginning the day by making breakfast for the number you sneaked in while I was asleep."

"I've already thought of that. We'll have house rules. No tricks under the communal roof."

"Fine," I said after a long swallow. "That means that if I should happen to meet someone I like: neat, clean, honest, hardworking, HIV-negative, I can't bring him back to my own apartment?"

"Come on, Geoffry, fair's fair. If I'm not going to drag anyone home, why should you?"

Had I not been so distressed by Larry's proposal I could almost have laughed. Larry inhabits a Ptolemaic universe in which all the planets, including Earth, revolve around him. How my own life might be hugely disrupted would never occur to Larry. Once he had decided the move was right for him, the only issue left to discuss was settling the date.

Much as I detest confrontations, I can only be pushed or manipulated so far. To share a flat with Larry would be to experience Sartre's theory that Hell is other people. My immediate dilemma was how to turn Larry down without turning him off; however, it is difficult being tactful with someone who wilfully refuses to read the signals. Were I not forceful and uncompromising, I would open my door one morning to find Larry and his suitcases on the welcome mat.

As if reporting on a summit conference that has already been held, Larry continued. "My schedule is more flexible than yours, so I can do the shopping. You're a far better cook so you can do dinner. With me paying half the shot we can eat out a lot. I drink gin; you drink Scotch, so we can each buy our own booze. It could be a gas. Come on, Geoffry, what do you say?"

What I should have said then was no, a no so firm and un-equivocal as to quench further discussion. I would far rather go onto welfare than live with Larry, but being a product, or a victim, of my Anglo upbringing, I fudged.

"It's a big step. I'd like to think about it for a while."

"If you have to think about it first I might be tempted to suspect the idea didn't blow you away."

Baffled, Larry didn't know how to react. He is a man of instant enthusiasms, a characteristic which goes far to explain his success in real estate. Without being dishonest he manages to find merit in the most tumbledown and ramshackle pro-perties, chatting up their dazzling potential so effectively that he usually makes a sale. I understood he found it difficult to grasp that I would fail to be swept away by what to him was a wonderful idea. How often during my youth I found myself in unpromising situations because the other person or people involved wanted something so badly that it seemed bad manners not to accommodate them. I slept with people I didn't much like and stayed late at boring parties so as not to appear a party poop. I drove miles into the country for meals, which always turned out to be chicken, only to be faced with a long drive back to the city in the dark. Luckily for me, I was still fairly young when I realized that deep inside the good sport I tried unsuccessfully to be, there beat the heart of a very poor sport. When you have been raised to be a good sport, to admit openly that you intend to please nobody but yourself is almost as serious as changing your citizenship.

As I finished my drink I could see Larry's fit of the sulks turning into a full-blown pout. "I'm going to have another," I said to bridge the widening pool of silence. "Another beer?"

"Bugger beer. I'll have a martini."

I confess to feeling a vague sense of relief. The sober, sensible, beer-drinking Larry was a product of role-playing at its most extreme. It was not unlike looking out the window one morning to see King Kong in the flower garden picking lilies of the valley.

It was not until Larry had started on his fourth martini, while I poked unenthusiastically at my egg rolls, that he again brought up the topic of our living together. For the sake of relative anonymity I had resigned myself to eating Chinese food, confident I would never return to the restaurant.

I signalled to the waiter and asked for a fork, then looked across the table to see Larry staring at my plate, his eyes two pinpoints of hostility.

"So what's so fucking precious about your life that it mustn't be disturbed?"

"Excuse me?" I sawed through an egg roll with the side of my fork to find steamed vegetables which had all the flavour of boiled wood shavings.

"I said why is your daily routine so goddamned important that sharing it with an old friend will bring you out in spots?"

I could see a confrontation coming, the way the dinosaurs

must have seen the giant meteor hurtling towards them out of the sky, but I made no effort to take cover. There was no point. Gin makes some people hostile, and Larry was no exception. I had drunk more than my usual ration of Scotch. Although not openly militant, I was not prepared to back off as I had done earlier at my apartment. I drew a deep breath and answered.

"If you really were the old friend you claim to be, you would know the answer to that question without having to ask."

It was a pissy answer, not designed to calm the troubled waters.

"What I do know is that you're not a well woman. Believe it or not, I can't read your mind – if indeed there is a mind there to read!"

I put down my fork. "I am fully aware you are not reading my mind because you are not moving your lips. But since you ask, let me propose a scenario. Picture a slow day in the real estate market. Not having much to do you will go to the chicken breast store to buy two chicken breasts, which you will virtuously bring home and put into the refrigerator. As is your custom, you will pour your first drink at five. By the time I get home, sometime after six, you will be bored with TV and hungry for company. I, on the other hand, will have spent the day dealing with people and would be thirsting for silence even more than a Scotch. On top of which I will have to prepare those chicken breasts: white vermouth and tarragon, a little green salad, rice or pasta. And during all this preparation, I will resent not only the sound of your voice but the very air you breathe."

"Well, shut ma mouf, Miss Scarlett . . ."

"Be quiet. I am answering your question. I know the sooner dinner is ready the less drunk you will become. It will take about

a month of seeing my dear little lamb chops overcooked to the
size and texture of walnuts, while you have one more drink,
before I say 'The hell with it! Why don't you order out.' There
will be no urgency about eating the food you have called in and
paid for, so you will proceed to tie one on. Jungle drums will throb
insistently in the distance, and you will head out into the night."

By now Larry's glass was empty, and he signalled for another.
"Go on. This scenario is soon to be a minor motion picture."

"You will meet someone in a bar. Naturally he won't have
a place of his own: he lives with his parents – his sister – an
unsympathetic roommate. You will remember your own injunction about no tricks under the communal roof. Another
drink and you will figure I am asleep. You will bring the trick
back home, past the all-seeing eyes of the night porter, and
sneak him into your room. After sex you won't even remember,
you will pass out. The next morning I will see a stranger coming
out of your bedroom, scruffy and unshaved, and asking whether
he might have a cup of coffee for the road. That is, if he hasn't
already decamped with your watch and wallet and my VCR."

Larry giggled into his drink. "Is there more?"

"You bet. After I have bounced you off the walls, you will
wallow in contrition, until the next time the jungle drums
begin to throb, and in spite of vehement protestations to the
contrary, you bring another of your street boys back home. I
would prefer not to spend my declining years in prison, but that
is where I will probably end up when the authorities learn I
have beaten you to death with the frozen leg of New Zealand
lamb you bought for the following night's dinner. So for both
our sakes I honestly believe it preferable we maintain separate
establishments. Now why don't we eat before our lukewarm

food grows cold."

Larry took a long swallow. "Up yours with chopsticks, Chadwick. I wouldn't live with you if we were fucking marooned on a desert island."

"Then we are agreed. You will continue to visit me in Montreal. I will see you when I come to Toronto. And we may go to our graves still on speaking terms."

"Don't bet on it, dickhead. I don't need friends to point out every time we have dinner that I'm a randy, drunken roundheel. And what about you, you pious prick. Single-handedly you keep the Scottish distilleries in the black, and you've spent more time looking at the ceiling than Michelangelo."

I burst out laughing. I love a good zinger, even at my own expense; Larry had scored. "Can I put that line into the screenplay?"

My laughter only seemed to rile Larry further. "There is nothing more tiresome than a reformed whore. When do you come on with the charity and good works? Face it; now that you've too goddamned old to make out you're obliged to fall back on virtue."

Perhaps I should have been offended; the observation was meant to wound. But the truth has an uncomfortable way of being true.

"You're right. Men over sixty are not a hot item in a culture that gets off on youth and beauty. As I see it, any number who will make it with me will make it with anyone. And people who make it with anyone are far more likely to catch those nasty little social diseases that nice girls don't get. You could bear that in mind. Heavy drinking and safe sex are like bubble gum and false teeth. You appear to have been lucky so far, but why push your luck?"

I guess that was an observation I shouldn't have made, but nobody likes being put on the defensive.

Larry drained his glass. "My luck ran out the second I reached for the phone and suggested we have dinner. Of all the shitty ways to kick off a vacation. I'm not hungry. Your sanctimonious face would put anyone off his feed. You could spoil a wet dream. If you will excuse me, I think I'll get some air." He pushed himself to his feet.

"There's a pharmacy about two blocks west of here. I think it stays open late. You may want to play it safe – little joke there. I think two or three dozen should see you through the evening."

In full view of the restaurant Larry gave me the finger. "It saddens me to think you have to put your dinner in that mouth."

"One word of advice, Larry, when you get down South I suggest you carry your spare cash in an outside hip pocket. It will be a lot safer than tucked into your underwear."

"Kiss my bee-stung ass!" And off he lurched, leaving me once again to pick up the tab.

I peeled the rubbery batter off a couple of shrimp, ate a few spareribs after wiping them with a napkin, and teased a few slices of beef from under pea pods. The bill for Larry's drinks came to more than his food, but I expected it. Even if we don't have a row I generally end up paying. I don't mind, as I see him only a couple of times a year. Well, at least I had put the idea of our living together to rest. So pleased was I to be let off the hook that I put an extra few dollars onto the tip. I don't honestly believe one can buy off fate, but a little appreciation never hurt anyone.

By the time I had taken a taxi home, past buildings all

tarted up with the tinsel trappings of Christmas and store windows blazing with coloured lights and aluminum foil poinsettias, my annoyance with Larry had descended into gloom. I did not relish the prospect of growing old alone any more than he did, but unlike him I could imagine the pitfalls of trying to share a limited space with someone incompatible. For all his having lived in the fast lane, Larry has gleaned little of life, that which was once called wisdom. He knows how to operate a computer and program a VCR without the instruction manual, but his idea of a good time is drinking heavily and going out on the town, just as when he was twenty.

To live with someone congenial, someone whose well-being you want as much as your own, is a heady experience. It also raises the ante. I understand there are people prepared to make any number of compromises so as not to be alone, but I am not one of them. My father used to say that understanding your own limitations was the beginning of wisdom. He was a wise man, my father, understanding enough to have accepted my not turning out the way he would have wished. I miss him still. I miss Patrick. And I miss the resilience I once had, both physical and mental, which enabled me to adapt myself to new people and situations. Maybe I am standing on the threshold of a larger grasp of life, but as I wandered through the empty rooms of my apartment, waiting for sleep, I would have traded all the wisdom in the world for the tactile presence of someone who mattered.

V

There did not seem to be much point in my going to the office on Thursday, other than for something to do. I had a few letters to write, odds and ends to sift through, some research on a possible incorporation, but nothing that couldn't wait until next week. Nobody except those in the retail trade wants to work on Christmas Eve. This willing suspension of the work ethic extends through the following week to end reluctantly on the second of January. Depending on what day Christmas falls, the economy can lose seven working days between Christmas Eve and that most tedious of festivities, New Year's Eve.

Perhaps I should have bestirred myself and escaped from Montreal for those ten tiresome days. But where and, not to mince words, why? You bring your problems along with the traveller's cheques and clean underwear. Dashing through the surf towards the camera, or strolling along a deserted beach under a carcinogenic sun, I would still be Geoffry Chadwick, bored, irascible, and longing for grey, inhospitable Canadian skies.

Patrick and I had talked about taking a Christmas Caribbean cruise – piña coladas, duty-free shopping, bus tours, the works. At first I found the idea of going to sea in a floating Holiday Inn alarming, but Patrick tried to convince me that was the whole point. We would be on a seagoing theme park where we would only have to unpack once. We even toyed with the idea of a gay cruise, but Patrick argued it could be dangerous; the ship might founder under the weight of all that jewellery. And the truly exclusive cruises would be filled with the retired elderly nursing their watered Scotches and arthritic joints. Far better to immerse ourselves in the apotheosis of the middle class, straw hats and paperbacks, sunscreen and synthetics, and the welcome knowledge that Montreal in the grip of winter and holiday hysteria was far away.

Shared with Patrick's buoyant presence, a cruise could have been a wonderfully ghastly experience. But sitting alone in the cabin drinking doubles is no way to visit the Caribbean. The alternatives – New York, San Francisco, a quick jaunt to London and Paris – would only have underlined my solitude in a strange city. Somehow it seemed easier to succumb to inertia and remain within the boundaries of the familiar.

Late in the morning, the red light on my telephone flickered. "A Mr. Townsend to speak to you, Mr. Chadwick."

"Put him through, please. Larry? Are you still in my area code?"

"Unfortunately, yes. I had a few little drinkies in a bar after I left the restaurant. I realized too late that the best place for me was my own little beddy-boo. By the time I got back to the hotel I was so bombed I forgot to leave a wakeup call. Guess what?"

"There's a plane en route to Florida at this very moment with someone who was on standby sitting in your seat. What now?"

"I can't get a flight south for a couple of days, unless I go to the airport and wait around. And you know what airports are like on Christmas Eve."

"Are you going to stay in Montreal?"

"I suppose so. I'm just as well off here as mooning around

Toronto. I'd like to take you to lunch – really, and this time I'll pay the bill."

"It will have to be quick. I still have my Christmas shopping to do."

"Aren't you leaving it a bit late?"

"I always shop late on Christmas Eve. That way I have the stores almost to myself. And last-minute shopping is only last minute if you have something terminal."

Larry offered to pick me up at the office around one, and I returned to clearing my desk. True to form he had made no reference to our contretemps last night. Larry lives his life in a continuous present, what happened yesterday conveniently forgotten. Perhaps it's just as well. Recriminations are pointless and generally lead to escalating strings of accusations, as many people facing divorce lawyers or palimony suits have learned to their dismay.

At noon I wished my secretary a Merry Christmas and told her to take the rest of the day off. I give her a Christmas bonus; she gives me a bottle of Scotch. We shake hands, and that is that.

There was a time in my life when I regularly spent Christmas away from Montreal. For some years, in particular those following the death of my father, I used to take Mother to Toronto so she could spend the holiday with Mildred and the grandchildren. Mother hated to go anywhere alone; as often as not she tagged along with a friend or neighbour when shopping for groceries. To leave the city limits was out of the question without a companion, travel agent, tour guide, porter, and attendant; all these duties fell to me. I could think of about four-hundred and thirteen places I would sooner spend Christmas than with my sister and her brood, and these locales include an abandoned coal mine, a disabled submarine, or Edmonton. But duty, that "Stern Daughter of the Voice of God!" spurred me on.

Hauling Mother off to Toronto allowed Madame to spend Christmas with her own family, and as Madame took a great deal of the responsibility for Mother off my shoulders I was anxious to accommodate her. She got Mother packed and ready to go, and once I had tipped the steward in the first-class railway car to bring Mother a vodka, pronto, the trip passed without incident.

Because of my work we generally travelled on the day before Christmas Eve. This proximity to the big day meant that family gifts had to be brought with us on the train. Mother disliked shopping and gave the children money, crisp new bills stuffed into envelopes and rapidly appropriated by my sister for safekeeping. While the children were still young I brought presents suitable for a visiting uncle, extravagant, frivolous items which the children adored and of which Mildred disapproved. She did not believe boys should receive dolls or young girls expensive cosmetics kits.

With the advent of Mother and myself, the house filled to bursting. Elizabeth, the older girl, was exiled from her bedroom to make way for Mother. Jennifer had to share her room with her older sister, while Richard, the first born and only son and the one to whose room I was assigned, had to crawl into a sleeping bag in the basement. Fortunately, he was still young enough to think it fun, especially with the expensive transistor radio I gave him, on which Mildred naturally frowned.

One Christmas stands out, as it turned out to be the last time I slept under Mildred's roof.

I can't remember what I put under the tree for Richard and
Jennifer, but I clearly recall giving Elizabeth a set of Ken and
Barbie dolls. I speak of some years ago when Barbie was still a
toy, before her apotheosis into a cultural icon or fertility god-
dess for the declining years of the Twentieth Century.

For once Mildred appeared to approve. I had not given the
dolls to Richard – they cost a fair amount (Barbie wore a be-
jewelled evening gown and Ken a tux) – and once Elizabeth
grew tired of them they could be passed on to Jennifer. Mother
handed out her money, only to have it scooped up by Mildred.
I sat nursing a hangover from the Christmas Eve party, and
George, Mildred's husband, withdrew to his study from which
he emerged only when absolutely necessary. The morning
yawned ahead until noon, when Mother and I would pour a
little Christmas vodka in honour of the birth of our Saviour.

My first inkling that something was amiss occurred when I
went up to Richard's bedroom, mine for the visit, to find
Jennifer sitting on the handwoven bedspread, weeping. One of
the good features about being an uncle as opposed to a parent
is that uncles don't have to be impartial. I have always liked
Jennifer the best, and as a result she always received the most
expensive gifts.

Time blurs the memory of what we said – most of what
children say, including first words, are not interesting – but I
learned that Richard and Elizabeth had shut Jennifer out of her
own bedroom for reasons they refused to disclose. I thought
their behaviour a bit heavy handed and, rather than ringing in
Mildred, at the moment banging around the kitchen as she
prepared the festive meal, I knocked on the shut bedroom door.
When no answer was forthcoming, I resorted to adult privilege

and opened it to find tall, solemn Richard and bossy, knowing Elizabeth pausing in what they were doing to turn astonished faces in my direction.

On the bed between them lay the Ken and Barbie dolls stripped of expensive finery. One glance told me what I had always suspected, that the dolls were genitally underendowed; however, Elizabeth was busily colouring Barbie's pubic area with a ballpoint pen. I seriously doubt there is anything in the parenting manuals to cover this particular situation. Certainly uncles were left floundering on their own. Thinking it might be a good idea to get some clothes back onto Barbie, I suggested dressing Barbie in Ken's tux and putting Ken into Barbie's gown so they could attend the Beaux Arts Ball. At ten A.M. on a hungover Christmas morning inspiration flags.

What I had not realized was that the ousted Jennifer had watched us all from the hall. Before I could dissuade her she went downstairs to tell her Mother that Elizabeth had done something to her doll down there, and Richard had helped. (Mildred discouraged nicknames – Jenny, Liz, Dick – even for the children themselves.) At first Mildred, busy with her brace of Christmas ducks, paid scant attention. But Jennifer, doubly resentful because she had been excluded from her own bedroom and the fun, persisted. Gradually it percolated through to Mildred that the dolls had been stripped naked and cosmetically enhanced with a ballpoint pen.

It was at this point that the faeces hit the cooling system. Had it been up to me I would simply have walked away from the situation and let Elizabeth do whatever she wanted with what were her dolls. Not Mildred. Hurrying upstairs uttering phonetic noises suggesting outrage, she seized the Barbie doll and proceeded to remove Ken's tux. "Take that dress off Ken!" she ordered Elizabeth. "Whatever will Uncle Geoffry think?"

"Uncle Geoffry says they are going to the Bozars Ball," replied Richard, not realizing that one does not answer a rhetorical question.

Aware that I was party to the felony, Mildred gave me one of her looks. Then her glance fell on the doctored pubis of the now naked doll.

"What on earth!" she began. When confronted by an unfamiliar situation Mildred tends to save the baby and the bath water but throw out the bath. In this instance she confiscated the dolls and marched out of the room.

I was caught in the middle. I had given the dolls to Elizabeth; they were hers to do with what she wished. I also felt the tug of adult solidarity, the unspoken bond that lines up adults against children regardless of right or wrong.

"I'll see what I can do," I said to the crestfallen children. "Jennifer, perhaps you could have kept your mouth shut!" The asperity in my tone sent the child back to the other bedroom in tears, which I felt were merited. I followed Mildred down to the kitchen. "Mildred, I think you're making an issue over nothing. Barbie is old enough to have public hair."

My little joke passed unnoticed.

"Really, Geoffry, I thought you would have shown more judgement than to give children dolls that can be undressed."

"Hold on a minute. When we were unwrapping presents you said out loud 'What a lovely gift from Uncle Geoffry!' Now, I did not pay the best part of a hundred bucks to have you kidnap the toys. You've already grabbed their cash. Just give me the dolls, and I'll take them upstairs. What the kids do to them is their business. And in case you haven't already found out, Elizabeth was born knowing the score. She has peeked at her pop through the keyhole, and rightly so. It will save you that embarrassing little talk because she will already be *au courant*. All children are curious about sex. It's perfectly natural, not a nasty virus they picked up in the school toilet. Remember your own childhood."

"Geoffry, what can you possibly know about raising children." Mildred untied one of the plastic trash bags filled with discarded Christmas wrapping and stuffed the dolls deep inside.

Wearing a bathrobe, Mother drifted into the kitchen. "Is there anything I can do?"

"Yes, Mother, there is. Go up to your room and shut the door. Stay there until I come for you." So angry was I that I failed to see the irony of sending Mother to her room, instead of vice versa. Her radar picked up danger signals and she withdrew.

"Now, Sister-from-Outer-Space, you are not going to discard those toys. They goddamn well don't belong to you." I do not ordinarily use profanity, but Mildred hates it. I tore open the bag and pulled out Ken then Barbie. "I bought these for Elizabeth, and she is going to have them."

"Well, you are not going anywhere until I have said what I have to say . . ." And away we went, straight into a donnybrook that churned up all the animosities dating back to childhood. The emanations from the kitchen must have reached to all corners of the house, as not a creature stirred, not even a mouse. Mildred opened her favourite Pandora's box of grievances, at the top of which were my deficiencies as an uncle. I was hung over, fed up with Mildred's stupidity, and bored to the point of tears with this foolish argument. It was then that I let fly with a vulgarity that even today still surprises me.

"Mildred, when I want to listen to an asshole, I fart."

"Geoffry, kindly remember that you are a guest in my house."

"Not for any longer than it takes me to pack!"

That ended the interview. I hurried upstairs, returned the contentious dolls to Elizabeth, banged on Mother's door, told her I would pick her up the day after Boxing Day, and went into Richard's room to pack. The episode turned out to be a watershed for Jennifer. She told, and the consequences went way beyond those she could possibly have imagined. I checked into a hotel, telephoned Larry, and the two of us went out on a three-day tear during which I discovered, or rediscovered, that nobody is ugly after two A.M.

In a state of satisfied, cathartic exhaustion I collected Mother and took her back to Montreal. Wisely she said nothing, and after a while the situation blew over, as it must. Although I did escort Mother back to Toronto on subsequent Christmases, I always checked into a hotel. This independence allowed me to enjoy the holiday. Merely not having to get out of bed at six A.M. to open presents was in itself a gift. I also took a leaf from Mother's book and began to give the children money, in the form of a bank draft so Mildred couldn't hijack it for safekeeping. And when she wasn't around, I slipped them some bills. I still do, in the form of a cheque.

After receiving all kinds of gifts I did not want, I finally suggested to the children that they each give me a bottle of single malt Scotch.

"Isn't that a rather expensive gift?" Mildred had once asked.

"Not when you consider what I give them."

Mildred put on her sanctimonious face. "Isn't it better to give than to receive? You must have read your Bible."

"No, I grew up reading novels."

Once again we ended in stalemate. But I drank the Scotch.

My secretary had no sooner left the office than the receptionist called to say a courier had left a package for me at the front desk. The firm of Lyall, Pierce, Chadwick & Dawson, employs a nubile female to take calls, welcome visitors in two languages, straighten up the magazines on the coffee table, and do the odd bit of typing. I would not be in the least surprised to learn she moonlights at one hundred bucks a trick. Men like her because she makes their red corpuscles swell, and women like her because they can condescend to her high-hearted vulgarity. Her hair, lips, breasts, and legs are all deployed with minimum coverage and maximum effect, to the point I once suggested to the other partners that someone wandering in by mistake might think he had found a massage parlour, not a suite of law offices. I was dismissed as a bit of an old stick and a terminal bachelor, with the result that her cleavage continues to dominate the foyer.

The giftwrapped parcel was the shape and size of a shoebox, although curiously light. I supposed it to be a Christmas present from a client. Back in my office, I cut the gold cord and sliced the red foil paper with my desk scissors. The box was indeed one for footwear, its lid emblazoned with the name of a local shoe store chain. I lifted the lid.

Inside lay two dolls, Ken and Barbie, both naked. The Ken doll had been neatly sliced into two vertical halves, from crotch to crown. Barbie had been cut horizontally across the middle.

Still trying to figure out what the grotesque offering might mean, I heard the telephone ring on my secretary's desk. Going into her office I lifted the receiver. "Geoffry Chadwick speaking."

"I just wanted to know what you thought about my Christmas present," said the now-familiar threatening voice.

"I'm with a client right now," I said, trying to keep my voice as neutral as possible. "Would you give me your name and number, and I'll get back to you this afternoon."

My answer caught the caller off guard, as there was a pause on the end of the line. "Very clever. I won't leave my name just yet, but you'll find out what it is soon enough. Would you like to end up like Ken, or Barbie?" The line went dead.

As I replaced the receiver I found myself almost shaking from rage, not apprehension. I hadn't been given time to say some of the rude things I had been saving up. It was now clear that the shoebox with its dismembered dolls was a serious threat.

Reaching for my Rolodex, I located the telephone number of a detective agency our firm has employed in the past. In fact it was through this agency, once called Patrick Fitzgerald Associates, that I met Patrick again, to our mutual astonishment. Pat and Geoff had expanded into Patrick Fitzgerald and Geoffry Chadwick, tacit acknowledgement that we no longer needed to keep our public and private lives in separate compartments.

Shortly after Patrick and I began seeing one another again he decided that perhaps he was getting too old to be a private investigator. With my support and encouragement he moved into home security systems and worked out of a separate office. In the meantime, his former agency merged with another and reincorporated itself as Ace Investigation Services Ltd., the logo a round eye not unlike that which used to flicker with a greenish light on the radios of my youth. I thought the whole package terribly drab, but Patrick assured me that a jazzy logo went better with a talent agency than an investigative one.

I dialled the number, identified myself as a former client, and asked to be put through to someone in charge. Because of Christmas the office was operating on reduced staff; after a brief delay a man come onto the line. "Brian Fraser speaking. What can I do for you?"

"My name is Geoffry Chadwick, and I may have a problem on my hands."

A brief pause followed. "Are you by any chance the Geoffry Chadwick who has a sister named Mildred?"

"The very same. Do you know her?"

"I did. And I knew you too. At the time I was using my other Christian name of Angus."

"Angus Fraser? Not the one I used to chaperone?"

"The very same, to borrow a phrase. I now call myself Brian Fraser. Angus is a bit too Bonnie Scotland for my taste. Makes me think of prize cattle. What's your problem, Geoffry?"

As succinctly as I could, I explained about my mystery caller, the threatening card, the sliced dolls. I also admitted my reluctance about calling the police. Brian Fraser agreed that I was not being paranoid and the time had come to take steps. I arranged to come by his office this afternoon at three.

I replaced the receiver and allowed my mind to drift back several decades. Brian Fraser, or Angus as he had called himself, had been engaged to my sister Mildred, and for a while it looked as though they might actually get married. To my lasting amazement, my sister had been a popular girl. Perhaps it is only natural for brothers to think of sisters as a rag, a bone, and a hank of hair, but I can still remember how much she had been in demand. What is sex appeal but energy, and Mildred had plenty of that as a young woman. Even today Mildred remains a high voltage woman; if only more of that energy could be siphoned off into productive channels.

I was still mourning the death of my wife and infant daughter when Mildred met Brian Fraser. I liked him immediately. To be sure, he did not face stiff competition. Mildred surrounded herself with a cloud of nerds and nitwits, supine young men drawn to her unshakeable self-assurance. A couple of her gentlemen callers tried to put the make on me, but common sense dictated I not graze in my sister's pasture. One young man in particular, all lank fair hair and art deco attitudes, prompted my father to tell the story of the shy sailor who went out with a girl for six weeks before making a play for her brother. Consequently, when Brian Fraser arrived on the doorstep wearing his unassuming masculinity like a comfortable sweater, he seemed like a blast of oxygen in a smoke filled room. (Back then almost everyone did smoke.)

From the vantage point of the nineties, for all its drawbacks a decade that has seen improvements in the way people view the world, Brian and Mildred seemed an ideal couple. Yet the Yellow Brick Road did not lead straight to the Emerald City. Brian and Mildred ran into roadblocks, none the less insurmountable for being unspoken. Mildred was a product of Westmount. Born in the community, she had attended private schools, been a debutante in a gown which made her look like a lampshade, and spent a winter in Geneva supposedly acquiring polish. Brian, on the other hand, came from a community on the south shore of the St. Lawrence River, or the Mighty St. Lawrence as it is called by real-estate agents promoting a house with a view. In the novels and movies of my youth a standard complication was that of a person from the wrong side of the tracks trying to move up the social ladder. How much more daunting to come from the wrong side of the river, particularly a world-class river listed in every grade-school geography book.

Small lapses in social protocol were adumbrated: Brian failed to place his knife and fork together on the dinner plate; he did not stand when my father entered the room; sometimes he preceded Mildred through the door. More dismaying, he had his own point of view and did not automatically defer to his elders on points of religion, politics, or education. When Mother admitted to using few herbs in cooking, including salt, Brian pointed out that salt was a mineral. Mother sniffed and retreated into wounded silence.

I liked Brian better for these supposed flaws and did what I could to aid and abet the courtship. One of my contributions was to act as weekend chaperone at our country cottage. Social decorum forbade young men and women to stay alone together without the supposedly inhibiting presence of a relative or older person whose function was to discourage sex. Many were the weekends the three of us drove north. I read on the screened porch while Brian and Mildred went for walks from which they returned with mosquito bites in the most unlikely places. With my nose in a book, or my ear to the small, crackling radio I appeared not to notice Brian sneaking into Mildred's bedroom. I was a good brother.

But even back then, under the fearless, forthright façade

Mildred flaunted, there lurked a fear of the unconventional. For some reason which was never given, she broke off the engagement. I am convinced to this day that she loved Brian, and I suspect she lacked the nerve to marry outside her tribe. No one was sorrier than I. Brian and I had become friends, and I rejoiced in the idea of a brother-in-law I genuinely liked. Mildred sold out, and she knows that I know which has not helped sweeten relations between us over the years. God only knows, we all have the right to make our own mistakes. But some of these mistakes can alter our lives. I firmly believe Mildred would be a different kind of woman had she married Brian. He would not have stood for her pretentious nonsense. As it turned out, she married a professor and spent her married life shoring him up. Perhaps that was the right choice, for her at least. It all happened such a long time ago that I suppose it no longer matters much.

A brisk knock at the door announced that Larry had arrived to take me out to lunch. "It's been over twelve hours since I last saw you," he began with a disarming grin. "And I'm starved. I know you're supposed to be hungry one hour after a Chinese meal, but if you don't eat the meal you're even hungrier."

"Didn't you have breakfast?"

"I managed a muffin. I really wanted to chew on the waiter, but he was too nimble. Where shall we eat?"

We decided to return to Larry's hotel, which serves an excellent lunch. In the cold glare of day, Larry looked definitely the worse for wear. I can remember when he could carry on full steam ahead for days with only naps to keep him going, but age catches up with us all. Little snow had fallen, and the dull gray of concrete and stone only intensified the garish glamour of Christmas trappings.

"It's a pity you have to go away alone," I said as we walked up Peel Street towards Sherbrooke. "Wasn't there someone in the picture for a while?"

"There certainly was, and I had high hopes. He was married, but the marriage was coming apart even before we met. His one hangup was that he insisted on calling himself bisexual, don't you know."

"A bisexual built for two?"

"And how! But all married men with male lovers call themselves bisexual. I guess it salvages their egos. Anyhow, he divorced his wife. She got the house, the car, the children – then he took off for Vancouver with a younger man. How's that for a putdown. So I'm right back at Go without my two-hundred dollars."

"I'm sorry to hear it. How will you spend Christmas?"

"Television, newspapers, magazines, room service – just what I would do in Florida if the weather were bad. I may go to the movies. I'll drink a bit. It will pass."

"I've been invited to what the Brits call a drinks party this evening. I'm sure I could bring you along. But it will be a straight crowd and you will have to cool it. Please listen to what I am saying. You will probably be bored, but no more than you will be in your hotel room. I'm not playing games; I'm not deliberately putting you into a situation where you can get drunk and behave badly only so I can gloat over your lapse. If you don't think you can handle it, please say no. If you embarrass me I'll wring your neck. *Voilà tout.*"

"You underestimate me. I can be a model of decorum when the situation demands."

"I don't want you to drown in decorum. I just want you to act your age, not your shoe size."

Larry tugged his forelock. "Yes, your way-way upness."

Over lunch, which turned out to be low key and enjoyable, I told Larry about meeting Elinor and how she came to be living in Mother's apartment. I was tempted to tell him about my threatening calls, but decided to say nothing for the moment. Larry would feel obliged to offer solutions, all of which I had already considered. It was difficult for me to talk about a situation about which I felt so ambivalent. After coffee and a brandy – it was Christmas after all – Larry signed the cheque and went off to his room to sleep off last night. I left the hotel, ostensibly to finish my Christmas shopping, but in reality to keep my appointment with the detective.

Brian Fraser had changed less than I would have thought possible, considering the amount of time that had passed. Always pale and freckled, with a reddish tint to his light-brown hair, now graying at the temples, his face had become creased and furrowed but otherwise looked much the same.

"You look your age, Geoffry, but well. I shouldn't imagine you have turned into the kind of man who relishes being told he looks younger than his chronological age."

"I don't. The evidence faces me every morning when I shave. When people tell you how young you still look what they really mean is that you don't look like the mummy of Rameses II in the Cairo Museum."

We laughed and years fell away. Brian motioned me to a seat in a small teak armchair facing the teak desk. From my attaché case I took the threatening Christmas card, the box with the pieces of Ken and Barbie, and the delivery slip from the courier company. Brian examined the items carefully.

"And you have no idea who this person might be?"

"None. I can't place the voice. One of the problems is that my law practice is devoid of drama. I work outside the courtroom, so it can't be a disgruntled felon bent on revenge. Also, I never play bridge, so it can't be an irate partner whose ace I may have trumped."

"I daresay," said Brian dryly, a faint smile curling the corners of his mouth. "Are you quite certain you have no professional enemies? Have you ever been, say, involved in a hostile takeover? Did you ever act as consultant on a company downsizing?"

"No, never. A couple of my partners assisted in takeovers, but somehow I missed out."

"Then we can safely rule out a disgruntled employee who may have lost his job directly or indirectly because of you."

"Correct."

"Do you have a telephone that registers the number of the caller?"

"No, I don't. I am always a year or so behind the current technology. I have a secretary to screen calls at the office. And at home, I only just traded in my rotary dial telephones. Please don't ask about the VCR."

Brian smiled. "I won't. And in any case, I am fairly certain your caller would use a payphone just so he couldn't be traced. Now, let's for the moment forget you are a lawyer, which is another way of saying perhaps the threats are not related to your professional life. Can you think of anything you may have done to provoke enmity? Have you ever helped the police in any capacity? Were you ever a witness in a trial?"

I studied the maple tree captured in the full blaze of autumn in the teak frame hanging on the wall behind Brian's head and suddenly I remembered something. "There was one incident," I began, "about seven years ago. I was just entering a Toronto bank, on Bloor Street if I remember correctly, when a man hurrying out of the bank bumped into me so hard I was almost knocked down. I recall saying something sharp, along the lines of "Kindly watch where you are going. Other people use this entrance." As I spoke I looked straight into his face, which was partially concealed by a hat brim and his coat collar. He swore under his breath and pushed past me into the street. Inside, the bank was buzzing with excitement; one of the tellers had just been held up at gunpoint, and the thief was the man who had nearly knocked me down.

"A police cruiser gave chase, and the felon was apprehended. As I had seen him up close, I was asked to make a positive identification."

"Did you testify in court?" By now Brian was jotting notes on a blue-lined pad.

"Yes, I did. The trial was over almost before it started. He had been caught with both the money and the weapon. The gun was loaded. It turned out that there had been a rash of bank robberies at the time, and the judge threw the book at him. Ten years in the penitentiary."

"Do you know where he was sent?"

"Kingston, I believe."

"What was his name?"

"Dwayne, I think. Dwayne Brown, or was it Black? Yes, it was Black. Dwayne Black."

"Have you heard anything from this Dwayne Black since he went to prison?"

"Not a word."

"Did you happen to hear if he was paroled?"

"I know nothing further about him. I flew to Toronto to give testimony and caught the next plane back to Montreal. I wasn't even there for the sentencing."

"Let me make some inquiries," said Brian. "I'll find out if he is still in prison, and perhaps the dispatcher from the courier company may remember something." He stood, straightened the jacket of his gray suit, and adjusted the knot of his navy polka dot tie.

"As soon as I learn anything I'll call. Does your mistrust of modern technology preclude an answering service?"

"No, believe it or not I have one. Will you be in Montreal for the holiday weekend?"

"I will. Here's where I can be reached."

I tucked the card into my wallet. "Do you suppose Dwayne Black is our man?"

"Not if he's still in prison. That's what I intend to find out."

I turned to leave. "How's Mildred?" he asked. "I haven't seen her in years."

"Very well. She's a widow now, as you may have heard. Her children are all grown up and launched. No grandchildren so far, at least none that I know of."

"I have two children – my wife died last year."

"I'm sorry to hear it."

"I also have two grandchildren in Halifax, unfortunately. I

won't get to see them over the holidays as it's my turn to mind the store. But I'll go down at Easter."

"A much better time of year to travel, believe me." I moved towards the door. "Perhaps when Christmas has been laid to rest we could have lunch, or dinner – and exchange carefully edited versions of our lives."

Brian smiled his wintry smile. "I'd like that. In the meantime we must deal with your unwelcome caller. You'll be hearing from me." He came from behind the desk to shake my hand and usher me out. Just as well, as I still had my Christmas shopping to do.

Every year I attempt to convince myself that I will make at least a minimal effort to buy original Christmas presents, and every Christmas Eve finds me ambling into the liquor commission to buy a few bottles of decent brandy along with an equal number of muslin gift bags dotted with seasonal symbols. Those who don't drink brandy can stow the bottle away against the time they might need a gift in a hurry.

Perhaps Brian would like a bottle of brandy, more likely a bottle of Scotch. Even as I pushed my shopping cart past shelves stacked with holiday liquor, I felt uncomfortable for having let my friendship with Brian slide. There was no reason for us to have lost touch. I did not break off the engagement. After the split we had met for lunch a couple of times, the occasional drink after work. But by then I was moving into a different phase of my life and going out a lot, meaning I was having sex with anyone who stood still long enough. Brian belonged to a different compartment of friends. I don't think he would have disapproved of my choice, but life in the fast lane takes up a lot of time. Many of my childhood friends, with their young families and mortgages and domestic concerns, seemed irrelevant. Visits to the bars, weekend lovers, and clever little brunches were more interesting than supper at the kitchen table in a welter of pets and children. Now that we are all in our sixties those domestic concerns are paying off with grandchildren and a sense of familial community. But I made my choice, and it is way too late for regrets.

I had teased Elinor about putting the best face on the fire in her apartment. Much as I disliked the situation in which I found myself, I had to admit it was good to have run into Brian again, after all these years. In fact, as I wheeled my four bottles of brandy and one of Scotch up to the cashier, I felt a rush of something very like goodwill. I had taken arms against my particular sea of troubles and rediscovered a friend to boot.

Having carried the liquor back to my apartment, I realized that since tomorrow was Christmas Day I had better pick up a few staples to carry me through the weekend. I headed out, walked the few blocks to the grocery store, and pushed my way inside. Had Jerome Bosch been painting today he might have set his vision of Hell in a supermarket on Christmas Eve. The aisles were thronged with affluent women filling their carts with last-minute items prior to the Christmas Day siege. Far from festive, the place reeked of desperation. As one of only two or three male customers I could have felt out of place, had I not been happy playing house as a boy.

"Why, Geoffry, fancy meeting you here!" barked a familiar voice, and I turned to confront my sister pushing a cart as though her oranges had been painted by Cézanne and her carton of eggs came from Fabergé. Mildred had pulled off the very English Canadian trick of managing to look smart without

being stylish, a result of never buying anything that will go out
of fashion. The look favours shoulders without padding, skirts
to the knee, medium-heeled pumps, and jewellery that looks
antique even if it is not. She wore her mink, one of those
serviceable coats which could pass for muskrat at a distance.
Around her shoulders she wore a silk square printed with
horses' heads, snaffle bits, and crossed hunting crops whose sub-
text was that leisure hours found her cantering around the
paddock or riding to the hounds.

"Even boys have to eat," I offered by way of an alibi.

"Well, you won't have to worry about tomorrow. There will
be masses of food. Elinor is cooking an enormous turkey; it was
the only one she could find at the last minute. She had to
borrow a roasting pan."

"I understood you were going to cook the Christmas dinner.
It was your idea after all."

"I was going to, but Elinor insisted – and she has invited at
least half the guests."

I suspected Mildred was glossing over the truth, and that
she had done a number on Elinor. I would make a point of
finding out this evening.

"Geoffry," Mildred moved closer, "How long have you
known Elinor?"

"Roughly four and one-half days. We met at Audrey's Christmas spectacular."

"I had lunch with Audrey, and that's what she told me. But
don't you think that's rather short acquaintance for subletting
Mother's flat?" Mildred has a way of framing categorical state-
ments as questions.

"Why?" I asked. "Has she started pawning the silver?"

"Don't be silly. But she was wearing one of Mother's robes."

"One that I gave her to wear because all the clothes from her smoke-filled apartment had to go to the cleaners. Now, if you will excuse me, I want to get out of his hell hole. I'll see you in an hour."

My few purchases looked almost lonely in the bottom of my shopping cart as I joined a checkout line in time to overhear two women speculating on how they were going to get through the next forty-eight hours. One had every available bed filled with family; the other was coping with a demanding mother-in-law in a wheelchair. I wanted to suggest they both head for the hills.

I lifted my milk, bread, cheese, and eggs onto the conveyor belt, then noticed an envelope which had been tucked under the loaf of bread. Thinking it might have been left in the cart by a previous shopper, I turned it over to see if there was a name. GEOFFRY CHADWICK had been printed in capital letters. I could only assume it was something from Mildred, possibly a leaden attempt to be whimsical, so I tucked it into my overcoat pocket before paying for my groceries.

During the short walk back to my apartment building I realized I hadn't spoken to Elinor about bringing Larry along to her party. Not wanting to forget, I took off my overcoat and went straight to the telephone. As I had anticipated, Elinor insisted I bring Larry along, but I had made the civil gesture. I was just putting the perishables into the refrigerator when I remembered the envelope I found in my cart. At the same moment I wondered why Mildred would bother to carry around an envelope addressed to me when she did not expect to meet me at the market. Furthermore, I was due shortly at Mother's apartment, where she could easily hand me whatever it was.

I slit open the envelope to find a sheet of letter-sized bond paper on which had been scrawled: DON'T THINK HIRING THAT MICKEY MOUSE DETECTIVE WILL MAKE ANY DIFFERENCE. THE RAIN IS STILL GOING TO FALL.

All I could think of was that I had been followed since leaving the hotel after lunch with Larry, first to the detective's office, then into the supermarket. At the same time, I remember thinking how few men had been in the market when I went in. Not a single one of them had been noteworthy, cut as they had been from dutiful-husband cloth. Whoever slid the envelope into my cart must have done so while I was talking to Mildred. Several women had rattled past, but I don't remember any men. Admittedly, I hadn't been paying attention.

The idea that whoever was stalking me had been close enough to touch made me distinctly uneasy. As I stood there, indecisive, wondering whether to call Brian, I was startled by the sound of the telephone. Bracing myself to let fly with a barrage of invective should it turn out to be my unwelcome caller, I was disarmed by the sound of Brian Fraser's voice.

"Geoffry, just wanted to let you know I made a few calls. Dwayne Black was paroled last month. I checked with his parole officer, and Black has to report in once a week. That means there's a strong possibility he may be the one harassing you."

"Whoever my stalker is, he has me under close observation." I read the letter which I was still holding. "Too close for comfort – to borrow the refrain of a popular song."

"Do you remember what Dwayne Black looked like?"

"Not really. Medium height, medium colouring, medium everything; quite unremarkable. And the episode was some years ago. He could easily have changed his appearance.

"It sounds to me as though he may have an accomplice." Brian paused to clear his throat. "I checked with the dispatcher of the courier company, and to the best of his knowledge the package was dropped off by a woman."

"That would explain why I don't remember any man getting close to me in the market. He wouldn't be the first paroled con to have a woman waiting in the wings."

"True enough. Now, are you planning to do anything out of the ordinary over the weekend? Are you going out of town?"

"No, I plan to stay right here. I'm due at a party nearby quite shortly, at my mother's apartment, in fact, and I'm also going there tomorrow for dinner. Other than that I plan to stay home."

"Good. The less you go out the less chance you have to be bothered. Keep me posted if you hear anything further. We may have to put you under surveillance for a while, but Christmas Eve is not the best time for dealing with the police. If necessary, I'll watch you myself, although I seriously doubt it will come to that. So play it close to the chest for the rest of the weekend."

"What does surveillance mean? Will you be trailing along behind me, breathing down my neck? Should we set another place for Christmas dinner, not that you wouldn't be welcome."

"No, no, nothing like that. I might park my car outside your building for a while. If you see a dark blue Toyota just ignore it. You won't be in the least inconvenienced. Just don't do anything out of the ordinary."

"A situation like this makes even the ordinary look unusual, but I'll stay on the high road. At the risk of sounding presumptuous, let me suggest that you take care. This guy sounds as if he means business."

I hung up, not feeling particularly reassured. Obvious to me was that Brian did not consider me in real danger. Up to now I would have agreed, but that envelope in my shopping cart made me realize how close my stalker, or his accomplice, had come, and also how unaware I had been of his presence.

VI

The buzzer on my intercom rang and the doorman informed me a Mr. Townsend was waiting in the lobby. Life continues, and I went down to meet Larry.

The doorman at Mother's apartment building knows me so well he did not bother to telephone Elinor for permission to let me go up.

"Merry Christmas, Sam," I said as I slipped him an envelope holding the seasonal gratuity for what I hoped would be the last time.

"Merry Christmas, Mr. Chadwick, and God bless you, sir." He pumped my hand vigorously and smiled a broad smile to reveal shiny new dentures the size and colour of piano keys. Unwilling to ignore my guest in this burst of goodwill, he gave Larry a matey clap on the shoulder. Always game, Larry grinned back. The two of us rode the elevator to the top floor where I rang the buzzer to Mother's apartment. Immediately the door flew open to reveal Mildred in beige crepe and a string of rock-crystal beads I recognized as belonging to Mother. The faceted beads shimmered with the nostalgic glamour of a bygone age, when sex was still considered sinful and innocent men fell victim to vamps, those heavy-lidded females who reclined on leopard-skin rugs in velvets and ropes of beads. Yesterday's siren is today's camp icon, and strings of beads hanging to the waist have gone the way of turbans and fringed Spanish shawls. Mildred had failed the test. In order to accommodate the string of crystals to the neckline of her beige crepe (the kind of dress a mother-in-law wears to a wedding so as not to clash with dusty pink bridesmaids) she had looped the beads twice around her neck, thereby spoiling the long, graduated line from shoulder to waist.

"Larry!" she exclaimed, shaking his hand. "Of course. We met some years ago in Toronto. So glad you could come to our little party. Please hang up your coat and make yourself at home. The bar is in the dining room."

Mildred has a knack for making you feel like a guest in your own house. She could make the Queen feel like an interloper in Buckingham Palace.

"Where's Elinor"" I asked, hanging up my coat.

"In the kitchen making sandwiches."

Larry followed me down the passageway. Elinor stood at the counter on which slices of bread were spread out in neat rows. Assisting her in the assembly line was a familiar-looking, petite woman in black slacks and a crimson blouse.

"Good evening," said Elinor's friend as we came in. "Are you the gentlemen from the escort service? I'm Amy Hutchins, and this is Elinor Richardson. I understand your agency is offering a holiday special."

"For the double date that will live in infamy," added Elinor. "Please excuse me for not shaking hands," she smiled at Larry, "but they're covered in mayo."

"I'm pleased to meet you, Elinor. And thanks for taking in a homeless waif."

"This is my gracious and lovely friend Miss Amy."

"How do you do, Amy." Larry shook her hand.

"Let me lead you to the bar where I can make you a drink," said Amy by way of greeting.

"Please don't bother," I said. "Larry and I know our way around a Scotch bottle."

"You see, Elinor," said Amy. "I told you to buy Scotch. Not everyone is happy choosing between sweet sherry and Dubonnet."

"Don't mind Amy," said Elinor. "She gets excited at parties. I set up a bar in the dining room. Pour yourselves a drink and go into the drawing room. Mildred will introduce you around. We'll be in shortly."

We went into the dining room, where my niece Jennifer was pouring herself a gin and tonic. She looked lovely in a silk dress the colour of old gold, her burnished hair twisted into a French braid. I introduced Larry Townsend to Jennifer Carson.

"You're Mildred's daughter?" exclaimed Larry as they shook hands. "The last time we met you were wearing a retainer. You certainly have changed, and for the better. I, on the other hand, look just the same."

We all laughed out of good fellowship, I also from relief as Larry appeared to be putting his best foot forward. I was re-assured to see Larry pouring a tall Scotch and water instead of mixing his customary martini. He might well end up dancing on the ceiling, but it would take him longer to get there. We went into the living room where Mildred was holding court. As she caught sight of me she sprang forward to make introductions.

"This is my brother, Geoffry Chadwick, and Lawrence Townsend from Toronto. I'd like you both to meet Mrs.

Richardson, Elinor's mother. Alan Hudson, a cousin of Elinor's visiting for the holidays, and this is Gregory, Elinor's son."

In the ensuing flurry of how-do-you-do's and handshaking I was able to size up Elinor's family. Mrs. Richardson, a small, energetic woman, has the kind of stern, angular face whose vintage was difficult to determine. With a daughter of Elinor's age she had to be in her late seventies, but the absence of laugh lines and a small glass of sherry sitting untouched on a nearby table suggested the humourless intensity that can carry people into their nineties. She wore black. I suspect she seldom wore anything else and probably needed a flashlight when she went into her closet to choose a dress. Her single strand of pearls had the sheen of truth and, after the fashion of her generation, she wore the family diamond rings in clusters.

She was obviously dying to wrench the conversation away from Mildred, and I afforded her the opportunity. "Well, Geoffry, we finally meet, after all these years. I was just telling your sister that I used to know your mother at school. I understand she has moved into Maple Grove Manor. I hear it's very well run and doesn't smell of . . . the way so many old peoples' homes smell. I really must get in to see your mother. Do you suppose she'll remember me, after so much water has flowed under the bridge? I have to thank you for taking Elinor off the street and putting a roof over her head. Particularly as she has reversed the trend, as it were, and moved from Toronto back to Montreal. All too often it's the other way around. I honestly don't know what the French are about, what with language laws and sign laws and strictures about being educated in English. I can remember when they used to know their place. My husband says he has seen it coming for years, but still . . ."

I find women like Mrs. Richardson easy to deal with. All you need to do is pretend you are listening, the occasional nod, an almost inaudible murmur of agreement, and your mind is free to roam. While her mouth was feeding words into the air I studied the men in the room, in particular Elinor's son. It was easy to see why he had women pounding on his door. He looked as though he had just stepped out of an NBC movie-of-the-week. Tall, athletic, well dressed, he carried a shopping list of attractive features: large hazel eyes fringed by luxuriant lashes, perfect teeth, a cleft chin, dimples, and large, well shaped hands. He shook my own hand firmly when introduced and called me sir. He deferred to his grandmother. Elinor must have done something right.

Alan Hudson, who seemed to have come with Mrs. Richardson, looked as though someone had telephoned central casting to request an academic type for a cameo. He wore grey flannel trousers and a Harris tweed jacket; a handwoven tie with a knot the size of an apple blended into the tattersall shirt. From the granny glasses to the rubber-soled Wallabies he was perfect, even a bit of a dandy with his carefully trimmed beard and well-groomed hair. Of average height, he carried no excess weight. I am sure women found him attractive.

At an earlier time I too would have found him appealing; however, I have dated more than my share of academics over the years. They eat for three and can stretch a dime to look like a dollar. In spite of working in what is supposed to be an intellectual hothouse, their favourite conversational gambit is academic gossip, of limited interest to anyone who does not know the people involved. And I have a short attention span when it comes to following textual inconsistencies through subsequent editions of *Hamlet*, or in the real causes of the Seven Years' War.

Mrs. Richardson sailed on uninterrupted. She is one of those women I remember from my childhood. Once they have started to tell a story there is nothing, not a silver bullet nor a stake through the heart, that will cause them to alter course. "We had our family Christmas last night, as my granddaughter is spending the weekend with her husband's family. On Christmas Day, I'll just cook a chicken for Mr. Richardson and myself. Elinor is going to roast an enormous turkey and serve dinner here, but my husband dislikes going out. Fortunately Elinor has invited Alan; he would be bored to tears with just Mr. Richardson and myself, and the turkey she has bought would feed an army."

Alan Hudson, who appeared to have overheard Mrs. Richardson's remarks, gave an all-purpose smile which could have suggested pleasure or apprehension, perhaps both. Possibly Mildred felt a little bit uncomfortable under my accusatory look, as she made a feeble attempt to justify herself. "I'm so pleased Elinor has volunteered to undertake the turkey. I've never cooked a bird that size. Now, Alan, let's sit down so that you can tell me in what faculty you teach. My late husband taught at the University of Toronto." Having snagged Alan, she steered him as far away from Mrs. Richardson as she could without leaving the room.

I turned around to find Larry, as I wanted to take him aside and warn him that Gregory Richardson was out of bounds, but he had sneaked away. As he was not in the dining room pouring a drink I went into the kitchen to find him laughing with Elinor and Amy. I could hardly blame him. The combination of Mrs. Richardson and Mildred was about as much fun as a trip to the dentist. Besides, the kitchen is the real focus of action at most parties.

Elinor spoke. "I've just met a man who was asleep when his plane for Florida took off. That's a first. If I had the chance to go to Florida I'd be all dressed and ready to go at five A.M." She laughed out loud, and soon we were all laughing with her. "Imagine being stranded in a Montreal hotel for Christmas. He's going to have dinner with us tomorrow. So is Amy." Elinor made a broadly theatrical gesture of pretending to conceal her mouth with her hand. "I had to invite her. She provided the roasting pan so I can cook the bloody bird."

"How come you have a pan that size?" I couldn't help asking. "Elinor tells me you have only one child."

Amy laughed. "It was one of those misbegotten garage sale finds. I had planned to use the top and bottom of the roasting pan as planters for nasturtiums. They looked even hokier than they sound, worse than an old bidet filled with marigolds."

"I still say you can't beat a row of tires planted with impatiens." Even as I spoke I realized the dinner party was growing steadily larger. "We'll be ten. "Won't that be a large number to feed?"

"Amy will give me a hand, as will Jennifer, I expect." Elinor had not mentioned Mildred, and I guessed there was a reason. Elinor cut the last four sandwiches in half and piled them onto the platter. "Let's see; there'll be you and me, your mother and her friend Walter Morgan. Mildred tells me he is one of your Mother's oldest friends and Mrs. Chadwick asked if he could be included. Then there will be Mildred and Larry, Amy and Alan, Jennifer and Gregory."

If I had misgivings I tried not to let them show. Cooking Christmas dinner for ten people is a large undertaking, and I didn't want to quench enthusiasm. I must have looked somewhat dubious, as Larry sidled up to me. He knows me well and couldn't resist a dig.

"Why the melancholy penumbra, Chadwick?"

"I'm not really here; I'm a hologram."

Elinor picked up the platter of sandwiches. "I'll put these on the dining room table and people can help themselves. Now, everyone into the living room and please sparkle."

As the two women left the kitchen I put a restraining hand on Larry's arm and dropped my voice. "I know he's gorgeous but he's off-limits."

Larry assumed an expression of mock offense. "Please, Geoffry, give me credit for a milligram of common sense. Emily Post taught me that when you are an uninvited guest you do not put the make on the hostess's son. It's not me you have to worry about but your niece. If you want my advice, she ought to be wearing a chastity belt."

"It's already giftwrapped and under the tree. Shall we join the others?" I was in no hurry to put myself within range of Mrs. Richardson, but with Amy and Elinor in the room the dynamics were bound to change. I picked up my drink and followed Larry down the hall.

To give Elinor credit, her Christmas Eve party was less awful than many such gatherings I have attended over the years. A fair number of people dropped in for a quick drink and to wish Elinor a Merry Christmas on the occasion of her return to

Montreal. It was evident that, in spite of having lived for many years in Toronto, she still had a great many friends here. Some people have a talent for making and keeping friends. I am not one of them, but I can recognize and appreciate the knack in others.

Presents began to accumulate under the artificial tree, all chosen from that list of approximately twelve items the good people of Westmount exchange annually. I suspect many of the objects go unopened into a bottom drawer to wait for the following Christmas. There was a compact disc, a shape impossible to disguise. With any luck it would turn out to be real music and not a safe assortment of easy-listening classics: "The Waltz of the Flowers," "The Sorcerer's Apprentice," and the humming chorus from *Madama Butterfly*. Another unmistakable box held After Eight dinner mints: chocolate covered patties each in its own tiny envelope. Just so long as the protective cellophane wrap remains intact the mints can be passed around for years. It is difficult to disguise a bottle of wine, no matter how many holly wreaths festoon the gift bag. Other packages may turn out to contain a tote bag sold in support of a worthy cause, or a cookbook whose focus is narrow: *Breads and Pastries* or *Low-Calorie Desserts*. Sometimes there is a gift-of-the-year, say pet rocks, Swatches, or wrist wallets that fasten with Velcro; but the hardcore stocking stuffers seldom change and offer a touch of continuity in a season where one dreads the unexpected.

Mrs. Richardson appeared to be enjoying herself, although I am certain she will tell her husband that making the effort to talk to all those people was exhausting. Her mouth was a fax machine, oblivious to her audience, tiresome but harmless. Whenever that audience grew restive or moved away, Mrs.

Richardson would leave the room on some pretext or other, only to re-enter with a pre-emptive bustle and capitalize on the eddy of attention she managed to generate. She reminded me of my sister. Both were warrior women, born to nurse the sick in appalling conditions, man soup kitchens, brave sniper fire to carry important dispatches. Instead of crisis, they found themselves trapped in safe, middle-class lives, their desire to serve and be splendid reduced to charity fundraising, budget-conscious shopping, and creative use of leftovers.

Mildred seemed to have taken quite a shine to Alan Hudson. Early in the evening she had cut him out from the herd and was riding close. Whether he was interested or merely being polite I couldn't tell. Jennifer and Gregory, the youngest people present, had retreated to the dining room to engage in one of those intensely serious discussions that is the first step in the mating ritual. They stood apart, heads bent, spines curved, trading opinions and eye locks, and barely looked up when I came in to make myself another drink. Youth is economical.

About to return to the living room, I was joined by Alan, like myself, in search of a refill. We fell into conversation, from which I learned he was recently divorced and that his children were spending Christmas with their mother. I suggested there were more alluring places than Montreal to enjoy Christmas, but he explained he wanted to spend a day at the McGill University library. This in turn led to his telling me he taught Canadian history and was researching an article on the evolution of Parliament. Like strangers learning they belonged to the same fraternity, we discovered we were both in favour of abolishing the Senate and a bond was forged. An interesting discussion might have ensued had not Mildred arrived in pursuit of Alan.

I must be getting older and possibly wiser. Twenty years ago I would have been more interested in learning whether Alan's marriage had broken up because he was gay than exchanging views on the Senate. How liberating it is not to be constantly on the make. Back when I was running around I believed myself to be free, all the time too callow to realize I was in the thrall of an idea. Promiscuity is not freedom, only another form of addiction. It took me a while to learn that ineluctable truth, but as we say locally, *Mieux vaut tard que jamais.*

To my surprise and relief, Larry appeared to be on his best behaviour. As he had accepted the invitation to return the following night for dinner I guess he didn't want to blot his copybook. At the moment he was exchanging ripostes with Amy in the hall. She followed me into the dining room while I replenished my drink. For the first time this evening we found ourselves alone.

"We meet again," I observed without much originality. "I told Elinor that we met some time ago, *nada mas.* I did not supply footnotes."

"Bless you for that." She rolled her eyes. "We all make mistakes in our lives, but that was one of my larger ones. Seeing Hartland was like having an affair with a mutual fund."

"I wouldn't know. But I was on the spot. His wife is a friend from way back."

"Will you accept a retroactive apology. I don't like involving other people in my lapses."

I smiled. "I hope he gave you a *bon voyage* bibelot."

"You won't believe what I got: a bowknot brooch studded with diamonds, tiny ones. I don't even know anyone I can give it to. You have to have one of those sensible, drab wool suits so you can pin it to the lapel, or else a black lace cocktail frock. I have neither."

"I'm glad to hear it. However, the less said the better, especially as Elinor is also a friend of Audrey's. Now, if I were you, I would go and vamp Alan, recently divorced and possibly up for grabs."

It was Amy's turn to smile. "You're okay. It's a long time since I've been able to look up to a man without lying down. Catch you later."

The water jug on the bar stood empty, and I carried it out to the kitchen for a refill. Elinor had just plugged in Mother's electric kettle. There was a time when any surge of power would have blown a fuse, but the wiring has since been upgraded.

"Thank you for looking after yourself," she said, "and not coming to wring your hands and tell me the jug is empty. Somebody wants coffee. A fully stocked bar and she wants coffee, very strong." Elinor spooned coffee powder into a mug. "She won't get to sleep before February. And coffee doesn't sober you up; it makes you into a wide-awake drunk. Are you surviving the evening?"

"Very well, as a matter of fact."

"Have you had any sandwiches?"

"Not yet, but I will. Some people never drive and drink. I never drink and eat. Why spoil a perfectly good high with food?"

Elinor shrugged. "I hadn't thought of it quite that way. Have you noticed how the youngsters seem to have taken quite a shine to each other? I only spoke with Jennifer briefly, but she seems very engaging."

"And in answer to the unspoken question, I have no idea

why she turned out so agreeable. We certainly can't blame it on the example she received from her mother."

"Why Geoffry Chadwick, I was thinking no such thing."

We shared a quiet laugh. "Elinor, are you quite sure you can cope with tomorrow's meal? I was under the impression that Mildred had intended to cook the meal herself, for Mother."

"She was, but – how can I put it tactfully. Let me just say I can put up with only so much stonewalling before I take over. Where does one go to buy a turkey? How large should it be? Should it be stuffed? What vegetables should we serve? Will there be a salad before dessert, whatever that may be. And so on. I'd rather do the job myself and have it done right. And several of the guests will be here at my invitation."

"I see. Just make sure Mildred pays her share. She tends to be frugal. She wouldn't pay a nickel to see an earthquake. Is there anything I can do to ease the burden?"

"Could I possibly call on you to carve?"

"Certainly. I haven't had much experience with a turkey that size, but I'll manage."

"I know it's sexist of me," said Elinor, "but I've always thought of carving as a male prerogative. I don't even like to try. Andrew hated carving, but I was firm. As a matter of fact, preparing for the meal has been a blessing in disguise; I've been too busy to mope."

"I wish I could say the same, but a little Scotch helps."

A woman padded into the kitchen in stockinged feet. Her French roll had begun to collapse, and her lipstick needed repair. "Is my coffee ready?" she inquired as though her jaw were full of Novocaine. "I'm the designated driver, but I'm afraid I took a detour into the vodka."

I smiled and eased my way out. Perhaps it would be a good idea to eat something. Then I could think about leaving. I went into the dining room to find Larry wolfing down a sandwich. "They're good," he said between bites.

"Will you be ready to leave soon?"

"Yes, and I want points. I just had to promise Elinor's mother that I'd make a special trip to Montreal for her church's annual Easter bazaar. I'll be able to find fabulous bargains on hand-knitted baby clothes."

"Be of good cheer, Larry," I said reaching for a sandwich. "The infants of today are the gays of tomorrow."

"You could run for Parliament on that slogan, with a platform of separate restrooms for the emotionally ambivalent."

"What kind of visual logo would you suggest to go with the little man wearing a suit and the tiny woman with her triangular skirt."

"Maybe the little man wearing the suit, and a big picture hat. I understand they're coming back." Larry reached for another sandwich.

"And heels?"

"And a stole?"

A couple came into the dining room in search of food. Larry didn't skip a beat. "So I said to the mechanic, 'Could I get away with steel-belted radials on the rear wheels for winter?' But naturally he wanted to sell me four new tires."

"Maybe you should think of buying a car," I suggested, reaching for a sandwich. "After this I'll find our hostess and say goodnight."

My announced departure precipitated a general exodus, no doubt to Elinor's vast relief as the following day promised to be a killer. Gregory and Jennifer left together. They had spent the entire evening talking to one another, but so far I had yet to see either of them smile. En route to the bar for a refill I had casually eavesdropped on their conversation. Gregory was explaining that he was involved in a problematic relationship; the young woman he was seeing made demands he was finding increasingly difficult to meet. He seemed to suggest the demands were emotional, but I'd be willing to bet cash she went at his bare body as though he were a pizza and she a hungry truck driver. Jennifer made the appropriate sympathetic sounds.

Mrs. Richardson stayed on until the bitter end. Since she had arrived with Alan she intended leaving with him, to Mildred's dismay. Elinor and Amy came to say goodnight.

"Do you really have to go?" demanded Mildred as she helped Alan on with his coat.

"It's late," replied Elinor's mother. "We'll probably have difficulty finding a cab. If we have to walk home, I would prefer to do so on a strong right arm. Elinor, it was a lovely party. Be sure to call your father tomorrow and wish him a Merry Christmas. Plan to come for a meal on Boxing Day. I have a little roast of beef which will be a welcome change from turkey. It's been a pleasure to meet you, Geoffry. Please let me know if your mother would like a visit. It's difficult to tell with old people. Some are simply starved for company, and others simply hate to be disturbed. Merry Christmas, Mildred. Please remember me to your mother. Happy holidays, Amy. Goodnight everyone."

And she took off briskly down the hall towards the elevator, leaving Alan to voice his thanks for the evening. For a brief moment he formed the apex of a triangle with Amy and

Mildred as the base.

"You'll be back in less than twenty-four hours," said Elinor. "Let's just say *au revoir*."

Larry and I were next to go. I offered to see Amy home, but she volunteered to stay and help Elinor tidy up. Elinor waited in the door until the elevator arrived. Larry and I turned to wave, and she blew us a double kiss. The night was not cold, and Larry and I walked along Sherbrooke Street to my corner.

"Was I suitably well behaved?" he inquired.

"Yes indeed. You surprised me."

"It was like the best of all Tupperware parties. Trying to dodge the awful mother turned it into a kind of game. Women like Mrs. Richardson teach you how to be a moving target."

"Do you think you'll survive tomorrow night?" I asked.

"Sure. I like Elinor, and Amy is fun, once you beat her off. She comes on very strong to any man who is not handcuffed to his woman."

By now we had reached the corner of my street. Larry's hotel lay east along Sherbrooke Street. "Larry, I want you to go straight home, back to your hotel. No rounds of drinks for Santa and the elves; no helping to deliver the toys. Home!"

"You're not a well woman. Who can get into trouble on Christmas Eve? To tell the truth, I'm still under the weather from last night. I'll call you tomorrow, but not too early. *Ciao*."

I nodded to the security guard as I entered my building. I didn't recognize him; he was probably a holiday replacement. Ordinarily I would not have cared one way or the other, but the regular guard was ultra sharp. He can tell where the bodies are buried and probably knows more about me than I would like, but he would also be quick to spot anyone or anything faintly suspicious. I rode the elevator to my apartment wondering uneasily if there would be a message from my mystery caller on the answering service. To my immense relief there was nothing.

I automatically switched on the TV, but found only the usual Christmas fare: seasonal music; *The Nutcracker*; heartwarming movies; and one of several film versions of *A Christmas Carol*.

I tried to read, but my mind kept wandering off the page. Patrick crowded my thoughts. To keep depression at bay I put on a videocassette of *Don Giovanni*, an opera both bracing and astringent. Mozart, like sherbet, clears the palate. My problem with the opera is that I really like the Don, even though he is supposed to be the bad guy. Don Giovanni turns tricks just the way I used to, only in his case they happen to be women – a thousand and three in Spain alone. Granted, I didn't have a manservant running after me keeping score, but when making out becomes your principal leisure activity the numbers pile up. The advantage of turning male rather than female tricks is that men don't come chasing after you crying out for vengeance and making scenes in public places. Conventional morality demands the Don be dragged off to Hell at the end of the opera, but that is where he truly belongs. Heaven would bore him to death.

I seriously doubt the Don would set much store by Christmas. In fact, he would probably be out getting laid on Christmas Eve while the other characters were piously attending midnight mass.

Patrick liked to attend midnight mass. I, on the other hand, never enter a church unless for a wedding or a funeral. Patrick didn't care; he went off to the midnight service, and I went to bed. Now he is no longer around to go to church, and I am unable to sleep. I wish it were otherwise, but wishes are not horses and beggars ride the métro.

I pulled my attention back to the Don, presently putting the make on a peasant girl. She is obviously intrigued, and who could blame her. The Don has much better legs than the bridegroom. I was only vaguely aware of the screen beginning to blur. When I awoke the opera had ended. And Christmas Day had begun.

The telephone jangled me awake. The clock said 4:05 A.M.

"You were out earlier," said the voice. "I kept getting the answering service. I just wanted to say I hope Santa Claus doesn't forget you because I certainly haven't."

I fought back the return of rage to answer calmly. "That's very thoughtful of you, Mr. Black. Now do you mind if I get some sleep?"

A brief pause. "I was wondering how long it would take you and that dumb detective to figure out who I was."

"Why are you doing this to me, Mr. Black. Harassing someone is not in the spirit of Christmas."

"If it hadn't been for your interference I wouldn't have been sent to prison. And things happened to me in prison that weren't pleasant."

"May I remind you that robbing banks is against the law?"

"It was your positive identification that put me away."

"I was under oath to tell the truth."

"You could have lied. If you had lied I wouldn't have gone to prison."

"You forget that I am a lawyer. And in spite of yellow journalism, lawyers do tell the truth."

"That may well be so, but the truth you told may well be

the death of you."

Suddenly I was unable to contain my anger. "Eat my shorts!" I shouted and slammed down the phone. Although it was late to telephone even a private investigator, I reminded myself I was paying plenty for Brian Fraser's time. I dialled the number he had given me and after an apology for calling at this hour, related the substance of the conversation onto the tape.

By now wide awake, I took aspirin and prowled the apartment waiting for drowsiness to come. Patrick would have known how to deal with the caller, unflappable as he was when confronted by problems that had me rigid with anxiety. He knew how to operate the VCR and the microwave oven. For my part I filled out his income tax returns and proofread important letters. Probably our two halves added up to more than a whole, but now that he is dead my half feels diminished – more like one third.

VII

Opening one's eyes on Christmas Day is just like waking up on any other morning, only today I slept later than usual as it was nearly dawn before I finally fell asleep. I switched on the coffee maker, only to be brought up short by the realization there would be no newspaper waiting for me on the doorstep. Sliding into the day with coffee and a newspaper is such a firmly established habit that to face the morning without one or the other gets me off to a rocky start.

I poured coffee into a mug that had belonged to Patrick. Across the front was printed "If you don't like the way I drive get off the sidewalk." I turned on the radio and picked up a *Messiah* in progress just in time to hear "Every valley shall be exalted" sung by one of those tenors who sounds as if his underwear were too tight. Then I closed the doors I had left ajar last night as I wandered about unable to sleep. As a rule I seldom went into the rooms Patrick had used. By now they had been cleared of anything personal and sat sparsely furnished and aggressively empty, like rooms in a college residence during summer vacation.

Patrick's former wife had, kindly I must admit, helped me sort through and clear out his possessions. She and Patrick had been high-school sweethearts, but no one should marry his high-school sweetheart unless he wants to live his life as a TV sitcom, the heartwarming kind. High-school sweethearts make their own strawberry jam and drive the neighbour's children to day camp. They feed the hamsters and help with homework. They volunteer for the United Church rummage sale even though they attend the Church of England. They do not give good head or exclaim happily over the size of their husband's cock when they are having Saturday-night sex.

Were I to permit myself feelings of guilt, that most self-indulgent of emotions, I would chide myself for not liking Lydia Fitzgerald more than I do. She is a worthy woman, deserving of respect and admiration. She dresses well and is not bad looking, given that high-school sweethearts tend to fade early. She has been helpful and understanding since Patrick died. She loved him too, and I know our shared love should create a bond. It doesn't.

Comparisons are odious – one of those home truths, like doctors being human, that I tend to question – but the temptation to rate Lydia Fitzgerald against Elinor Richardson was overwhelming. (Into such trivial channels does my mind drift when I suffer from newspaper deprivation.) Both women are about the same age; both come from solidly middle-class families; both had married a second time. The resemblance ended there. Lydia has dyed her hair a deep chestnut, throwing every puff and wrinkle into sharp relief. Elinor's pale silver hair compliments her face and highlights her remarkable green eyes. Lydia's clothes fit snugly at the waist, not a good idea with the encroachments of the middle years. Elinor's clothes fall from the shoulders, making a waist irrelevant. Lydia gets things done, but at what expenditure of energy. Watching her work is to drown in small sighs of effort and soft-focus exasperation.

Were she to be cooking Christmas dinner for ten, she would have to start planning shortly after Labour Day. I am the first to admit none of her defects is anything but minor; however, she lacks the tiniest leaven of humour or irony. Hers is a literal world: words have definitions; two and two add up to four; taxes and death will claim us all. I am unable to make her laugh, but she smiles at babies, kittens, and those stuffed toys which turn carnivorous predators into cuddly crib mates.

Small matter. She is now happily married to the right man. A perfectly matched pair, they are like bookends, shoring up the lives of his children by a previous marriage and two pairs of ageing parents. For Lydia there was a happy ending. About Elinor I am less certain. I hardly knew Andrew Ross, but if he was prepared to marry Elinor a second time, I'll bet she had his number in bed. Sex with her would be easy and fun; she gives off that aura. Finding oneself a widow in middle age cannot be easy. I could almost be sorry I am not straight. If I were, Elinor is the kind of woman I would court. The leopard cannot change his spots but, given the opportunity, would he want to?

I was in my early thirties when I had my last affair, with a woman that is. With mild amusement I observe today's gays, busy setting up archives to record gay history but afflicted with short memories. Most of them cannot remember or refuse to acknowledge a time when homosexuality was a truly serious stigma. Even my father, far more tolerant than most of his generation, used to joke that the only thing worse than being caught in bed with a dead woman was being found in bed with a live man. Girls were a given, and I adapted. Adolescence rhymes with tumescence, and way back then, when thinking about sex occupied most of my waking hours, I took whatever opportunities I could find.

Although it wasn't until after my wife was killed that I burst out of the book-lined closet, I still continued to have occasional liaisons with women. I was not an obvious fag, and the social courtesies had been drilled into me since I learned how to walk. Women continued to find me attractive, and there were times when the right combination of opportunity and alcohol had me tumbling into the feathers with a member of what my father's contemporaries called "the fair sex."

It was a term of approval, but sex is seldom fair. I met Claire at a punch party given by mutual friends. Sociologists today spend a lot of time and ink examining drugs, but few have bothered to investigate punch, the crack cocaine of my generation. Punch enables you to imbibe a large quantity of alcohol without realizing you are doing so. The base of ginger ale or fruit juice, often both, conceals the faint flavour of vodka or white rum with the result that you knock back cups of a cold, sweet, but not thirst-quenching drink garnished with slices of lemon and soggy strawberries. You continue to sip and end up drunk before you realize you are tight. Marriages have crumbled as a result of punch parties. Engagements were broken off, budding relationships severed. Punch has also been responsible for propelling often unlikely people into bed. Such was the case with Claire and me.

She lived in Ottawa and worked in the civil service. Recently divorced, childless, she seemed to want nothing more from me than I was prepared to offer, an occasional night out when she came to Montreal. I was not faithful to her and I assumed she saw other men. It was less an affair than an arrangement, nothing more. She dressed with style; without being conventionally pretty she understood makeup. She laughed easily, knew lots of government gossip, and kept me entertained over dinner. We drank a lot, and gin has always encouraged nookie.

We saw each other for a few months, always in Montreal, until one weekend I decided to visit Ottawa. An exhibition of Old Master drawings at the National Gallery was about to close. I telephoned Claire and asked her to have dinner with me Friday night. I planned to visit the exhibit Saturday morning, returning to Montreal Saturday afternoon. I also let drop that Friday was my birthday, a confession I should never have made.

Friday afternoon I drove to Ottawa and checked into a hotel. I fully expected to spend the night with Claire, but a hotel room is an escape hatch. At seven o'clock I rang the bell of her apartment, and the door burst open to reveal a roomful of strangers all calling out "Surprise! Surprise! Happy birthday! Surprise!"

More than just surprised, I was stunned. Strange men wrung my hand. Women whose names I did not know kissed me. (We called it French kissing then, blaming our lapses on other nations.) To begin with, the party was supposed to be in my honour but I knew nobody in the room besides the hostess. There was no Scotch or gin, only rye, rum, or warm beer. I suspected that Claire was using my birthday as an opportunity to pay off social obligations. We ate something that included hamburger, green peas, and a great many noodles. At one point she gave me a museum watch, one of those designer jobs with a black dial and a gold dot where the numeral 12 should be. I felt more embarrassed than grateful.

By the time the last guest peeled away I was tired without being sleepy. To be confronted with a roomful of people you don't know can be demanding and not nearly so much fun as is generally supposed. Hell could easily turn out to be a surprise party, any party, lasting for eternity.

Claire looked around the apartment, dismissed the wreckage with a wave, and suggested we turn in. I remember when I kissed her she tasted of rye, not my flavour-of-the-month. We got it on and she fell asleep. The only woman I could actually fall asleep beside was my wife. After a restless night, I dozed off at dawn.

It was close to nine when I awoke. I made instant coffee, showered, and dressed. By the time Claire surfaced, looking the worse for wear, I was ready to leave for the gallery.

"I was hoping you'd help me return the dishes," she began, putting on the percolator.

"Dishes?"

"The ones I borrowed for the party. They're awfully heavy."

Trapped by the code of conduct on which I had been raised, I had to comply. "I really want to get to the gallery," I said. "So while you get dressed I'll wash up."

Claire was still far from ready by the time I had washed, dried, and packed the borrowed plates and glasses into bags.

"Why don't I drop these off on my way to the gallery?" I suggested. "Then we can meet for lunch."

"No, no, I'll only be a minute."

Some time later a taxi came to collect Claire, me, and the dishes. "I have to stop at a florist," she said. "I want to buy thank-you flowers for having borrowed all this stuff."

I looked at the black face of the watch I felt compelled to wear. It registered what looked like half past ten.

While the cab waited, Claire hovered in an agony of

indecision between white roses or red carnations. I cast a vote
for the roses; she decided on the carnations, then realized she
had forgotten her wallet. "Let me," I said, beginning to sweat
with impatience and frustration. At the house of the couple
who owned the dinner service we were invited in for coffee. I
said thanks, but we had to go. Claire, who could not walk three
city blocks without stopping for coffee begged me to stop for a
quick cup. The cab waited while the two women held a post
mortem on the party.

By the time we got to the National Galley and I had paid a
staggering cab fare, the hand on my watch read twenty-five
minutes to the gold dot. I paid our entrance fee, waited for the
elevator while Claire went to the restaurant in search of coffee,
and found myself with twenty minutes to visit the exhibition.
By then I was so angry I could barely see, and when a guard
announced closing time I felt almost relieved.

My diffidence over lunch prompted Claire to do a schtick
that women in general should avoid. She pushed her voice into
her head and put on a little girl manner that made me want to
slap her. She flirted outrageously and insisted I couldn't be
angry with her over a few old drawings. My subversive self
wanted to tell her to fuck off, but my early training obliged me
to say I had, in that twenty minutes at my disposal, seen all I
wanted to. My goodbye outside the restaurant was civil but
curt. I went back to my hotel, checked out of my expensive un-
used room, and drove back to Montreal in a dark brown mood.

The situation did not end there. The following week a
catalogue of the exhibition arrived by courier. Then, to my
astonishment and dismay, Claire arranged to have herself
transferred to Montreal for six months. It became evident she

had an agenda, and I was it.

I did not want any further involvement with Claire and pointedly avoided her. I also realized that relationships with women could never be as clean cut and hard edged as those with men. I chafed over playing at romance. I resented being manipulated. I did not want to raise hopes without ever intending to follow through. The time had come to declare myself unequivocally gay and to remain on my own side of the fence. It is a decision I have never had cause to regret.

I continued to wear the watch until one afternoon I read 3:15 as 2:15 and missed a plane to Toronto. Shortly after that, Mother asked if I had anything to contribute to the gift table at her annual church bazaar. I considered it a sign from God.

A sudden surge of purpose sent me to my portable typewriter. When better to write a Christmas letter or two than on Christmas Day. It is curious how the birthday of Christ sends people to their typewriters, word processors, or Mont Blanc pens in order to chronicle what they have accomplished during the past year. Possibly the Christmas hysteria forces people into trying to make sense of their lives, to impose some sort of narrative structure on the barely controlled chaos that passes for daily life. No other major holiday, not Labour Day, Canada Day, or Rosh Hashanah causes this flurry of mail. Even vacations, major opportunities for taking stock, generally produce only a post card. "Having wonderful time. Wish you were here. Our porthole marked with an X." Hardly missives that are the product of self-scrutiny.

No sooner had I inserted a sheet of paper into the typewriter than the telephone rang. Uncertain of who it might be – Dwayne Black, the detective, or someone innocuous wanting to wish me season's greetings, I reached for the receiver. It was Mildred inquiring what time I would be picking Mother up. I replied that I hadn't known I was to collect Mother. Wasn't it Mildred's party? Yes, but I had a car and I was a man. Mother would feel more secure about leaving Maple Grove on my arm. I suggested Mother might feel even more secure were she to stay put and eat her turkey dinner in the Maple Grove dining room. Why must I always make difficulties, demanded my sister. If it was too much trouble for me then she would fetch Mother herself, in a taxi. Not wanting to see Mother used as a pawn in a family quarrel, I agreed to collect her around six.

"That will be fine," said Mildred in her victory voice. "Elinor is planning to serve dinner at seven and we don't want a long drinking hour. You know what Mother is like."

"Yes, I know what Mother is like, which obviously you do not. I'll have her there shortly after six. Oh, and Mildred – Merry Christmas."

I hung up before she had a chance to reply. In a curious way I was almost grateful to Mildred. Her ungracious call forced me back into facing the demands of the day. My immediate problem was to navigate the shoals of this dinner party, the Scylla of my sister and the Charybdis of Mother and her vodka. On a scale of one to ten, the problem of my stalker became much less significant when I thought of the potential for social disaster that lay ahead.

Around half-past twelve Larry called. "Merry Christmas, Chadwick. I've been up since the crack of noon. I wasn't drunk when I went to bed last night with the result that I haven't felt this good in years. I fought down the urge to kick off the day with a tiny triple and ordered breakfast instead. Another couple of days under your influence and I'll get religion."

"And a Merry Christmas to you, Mary Poppins. As a Christmas treat I'm going to give you the opportunity to make one of your cheesier jokes. You may just be out of bed, but I was up at the crack of dawn."

"And Dawn loved it! Thank you. The oldies are still the goodies. What's the drill?"

"As a matter of fact, you could do me a favour. I'm supposed to pick up Mother at her residence and deliver her for dinner. She's tottery at best and apprehensive about leaving the building. With you on one side and me on the other she'll feel a lot safer."

"Sure thing. What time shall I come over?"

"Say around five-thirty. How will you spend the afternoon?"

"I may phone in a movie. There's a pool. I can ride the stationary bicycle."

"Why not. You've been peddling your ass for years."

"Gee, Geoffry, I've never heard that one before. Five-thirty. And I promise to arrive sober."

After hanging up the phone, I thought it might be a good idea to check in with Brian Fraser, who I would have expected to call me back about the message I had left on his tape. Once again I got his answering machine, so I simply left my name and the time of my call. I also said that later in the day I would be at Mother's apartment and gave the number.

Next I dialled Mother's apartment. Predictably, Mildred answered.

"Oh, it's you again, Geoffry. I can't talk just now; I'm setting the table."

"I called to speak to Elinor, if you'll put her on."

Still holding the receiver Mildred brayed, "Elinor, it's Geoffry, for you!" It is certainly not by example that Mildred's children had learned to speak in modulated tones.

Elinor came on the line. "Geoffry, Merry Christmas. What can I do for you?"

"Merry Christmas, Elinor – more important, what can I do for you? Is everything under control?"

"More or less. Would you like to come over for a sandwich? There are plenty left over from last night."

Suspecting that Mildred was probably listening to Elinor's end of the conversation, I asked. "Would you like me to come over? Yes or no?"

"Yes."

"I'll be there as soon as I can."

"One more thing, could you bring some wine, if you happen to have any? Either colour. I'll be glad to replace it next week."

"Sure thing." As I had already showered and shaved, it took me only moments to dress. I packed two bottles of white and three of red into a bag. As the day was not cold I had intended walking over to Mother's apartment, but five bottles of wine weighed a fair bit, so I took my car. Few people were out, mostly those with dogs, which must be walked rain or shine, day or night, 365 days a year. I found a parking space across the street from Mother's building and rode the elevator to the top floor. Mildred answered the door wearing a large apron and a bandanna folded into a triangle and tied around her head, knotted at the nape, as though she were about to wash windows and beat carpets.

"Merry Christmas, Geoffry." She proffered a cheek to kiss.

"Dear sister." I hung up my coat and went into the kitchen. "Merry Christmas, tenant."

"And to you, landlord. Oh, good, you brought wine."

"And a corkscrew." I held out one of those folding corkscrews, favoured by waiters in restaurants, that looks not unlike a Swiss army knife. "I wasn't sure whether Mother even has one. Like Dracula, she never drinks – wine."

"Geoffry," Elinor lowered her voice, "would you be good enough to look at the dining room table?"

I pushed my way through the swinging door into the dining room. Leaves had been added so the table could accommodate ten. Places had been set after a fashion, with stiff, rectangular place mats treated to resist heat, stains, liquids. Six of these mats were decorated with Currier and Ives winter scenes, the remaining four with Redouté roses. On each of the mats had been placed an ironstone dinner plate from the service that was used in the kitchen.

Elinor came to stand beside me. "I wanted to use your Mother's Aynsley and the lace runners, but I was overruled. Gravy will stain the lace and the dishwasher will damage the gold border on the good china, which has been earmarked for Jennifer. A confrontation was brewing when you called. Maybe you could handle it. If you would prefer not to, I will, but I have not put in this much time and effort to serve my dinner on goddamned ironstone."

Ordinarily I might have attempted diplomacy, but today I was in the mood for a good donnybrook. "Elinor, leave it to me." I went to stand in the dining room doorway. "Mildred," I called, "will you come here a minute please?"

My sister came down the hall. "The apartment hasn't been touched since Mother moved out." She managed to turn the observation into an accusation.

When dealing with people like Mildred, attack is the best defense. "Did you set this table?" I demanded. "It looks as though we were expecting ten kids for a riotous birthday party. Why can't we use Mother's good china?"

"There'll be so many dirty dishes with ten people, too many to wash by hand. And the dishwasher is dreadfully hard on good china."

"So what. This will probably be Mother's last meal in what was for many years her home. Elinor is spending her day cooking the meal you dreamed up. And you want to deny us all the pleasure of an elegantly set table."

On the defensive, Mildred bristled. "Well, who's going to notice – when the plates are covered in food."

"I am going to notice. Elinor will notice. Walter Morgan will certainly notice. And if Mother isn't too drunk she will notice. As far as I'm concerned that makes a quorum."

"Geoffry. Elinor and I can manage quite nicely without your butting in."

"Well, my dear sister, I am butting in. I am going to set the table. Just remember, you are Elinor's houseguest, nothing more. And if you give either of us any flack, so help me God, I will telephone the *Toronto Star* and tell them the Blessed Virgin Mary was sighted on your front lawn."

As Mildred retreated into hauteur, Elinor burst out laughing. Nothing knocks a person off her high horse like the subversive power of laughter. Carrying her can of Pledge and rag as though they were the sceptre and orb, Mildred withdrew. In short order, Elinor and I cleared the table and began to set it to suit ourselves.

Seated at the kitchen table, Elinor and I ate sandwiches and drank tea. Mildred had taken a tray into the den so she could watch the Queen deliver her Christmas message on TV. Elinor opened the oven door, allowing the rich cooking odours to escape.

"I think our turkey is doing nicely."

"You know something, Elinor? Every politically correct bone in my body rebels at calling that poor unfortunate bird a turkey. There he lies, cooking away, no special interest group to lobby on his behalf, and you refer to him by that frankly denigrating term. Turkey indeed!"

"What would you suggest?"

"How about 'poultry of size'?"

"I'm of several minds about that one, Geoffry, all of them closed. I shall continue to call the bird a turkey, but in deference to your feelings I'll lower my voice."

After we had shared a quiet laugh, I asked Elinor about her plans after the Christmas holidays had been laid to rest.

"I don't know what I'm going to do. I hate to sound like one of those passive females who slink about in a chador wrapped to the eyeballs, muttering, 'It is written,' but I believe things have a way of working themselves out. Actually, I have a lot to do, like finding myself a permanent place to live and settling in. I'd like to find a job. I had intended going back to work before I married, or remarried, Andrew, but that was six years ago. A tight labour market plus my venerable age could make finding a job difficult." Elinor laughed out loud. "And as long as I get suckered into projects like cooking Christmas dinner for a woman I've never met, the time will not hang heavy."

"I'm sure there must be some sort of a support group for well-meaning widows without a strong sense of self-preservation who find themselves painted into corners. They teach you to walk on wet paint. Seriously though, are you sorry you volunteered, or were conscripted?"

"No, I'm not. I'm pleased to be doing something for you and your mother. You pulled me out of a hole. You have no idea how discouraging it is to come home from a party and see smoke pouring out of your apartment. Gregory is coming. Alan and Amy, both of whom are on their own. Last but not least, Christmas Day can be a real downer. So on balance, no, I'm not sorry."

Elinor finished her tea. "Now I must shower and change. Once the countdown begins I won't have time."

"Anything you would like me to do in the meantime?"

"Yes. You might set up a bar in the front hall. I don't want people in here making drinks while I am doing all that last minute stuff."

Setting up the bar was a pleasant task, an agreeable make-work project. I buffed the glasses with a clean dishtowel before lining them up on Mother's large Sheffield tray with its four baroque legs. A bar is welcoming; to see a bottle of Scotch the first thing upon entering, a good omen. Nowadays white wine is the drink *de préférence*, but I do not like white wine, even with fish.

The little contretemps over setting the table had driven other concerns out of my mind. By now Mildred had retreated to her room to dress. As the den stood empty, I telephoned Brian Fraser to report in, as it were, only to be answered once again by his machine. I checked in with my own answering service to learn if I had received any messages, but no one had called. I felt adrift. If only Brian had assured me everything was under control I would have felt better. In the beginning there was the word, and there are times when each of us needs a word, be it of reassurance, sympathy, or approval. Those comforting words tend to dwindle as one gets older. Children float through childhood on a sea of encouraging words. They also find twenty-five cents under their pillow whenever they lose a tooth. When a grownup loses a tooth he finds a dentist bill for five hundred dollars in his mailbox. Children enjoy long vacations without ever having worked a day in their lives. And they get genuinely excited over Christmas. I would not willingly be a child again, but innocence, known by some as stupidity, does have its advantages.

Elinor came down the passageway wearing a full black skirt and a white blouse with a softly rolled collar. From each of her gold hoop earrings hung a tiny blown-glass ball in honour of the season. She had taken extra care with her makeup, prompted less, I suspected, by vanity than by the impulse that causes a goalie to don a mask, that of protection.

"This is the nineties version of the maid's uniform," she began. "Actually I feel like a chorister from an *a cappella* group, but my only other dress is pale green silk; one spot of gravy or Hollandaise and it's off to the cleaners."

"That didn't take you long. Some women take hours to dress."

"Not if they are single mothers without live-in help. Thanks for setting up the bar."

"My pleasure, especially as I will be a frequent user. I should be getting along. Larry is going to meet me at my apartment, and together we will fetch Mother."

Before Elinor could reply the buzzer rang. Almost by reflex I picked up the receiver to be told by the doorman that a Mr. Walter Morgan was waiting in the lobby.

"Please ask him to come up." I put down the receiver. "Elinor, we are facing what every hostess fears more than a collapsed soufflé, the early guest. Dollars to doughnuts Mother gave him the wrong time. But I have a solution. If you don't mind me dining as I am instead of wearing a suit, I will deal with Walter and you can get on with your meal."

Elinor gave me the sign and I opened the door just as Walter Morgan stepped off the elevator. Small, shiny, wrinkled, he could have passed for a Santa Claus elf enjoying the night off. Impeccably dressed in a Prince Albert, he lifted his Homburg with the hand not holding the Hallmark Christmas bag filled with gifts.

"I hope I'm not early," he began, masking his anxiety with a determined smile, "but Constance – Mrs. Chadwick – said she wasn't sure what time we were invited, five or six. She said I had better come at five so as not to be late."

"Happy holidays, Walter," I said, ushering him inside. "It's all very relaxed, as you can see." I indicated the pullover I was wearing. "I'd like you to meet Elinor Richardson, our hostess – with the mostess."

"How do you do, Mr. Morgan. Let me take your coat. Please go into the living room and take the most comfortable chair. Geoffry will make you a drink."

"I am early," he said, immediately aware the living room stood empty. "And I do apologize. I should have telephoned, but I do so hate to disturb people on Christmas Day."

"Not to worry, Walter," I said. "We're very laid back. What can I get you to drink?"

"Nothing at the moment, thanks, Geoffry."

"I have to make one quick phone call. Please excuse me." I ducked down to the den and telephoned Larry's hotel. Luckily he had not yet left the room and I explained there had been a slight change of plans. Would he pick me up at Mother's apartment.

Going back down the hall, I paused at the living room door. Walter seemed to be listening to music only he could hear. He was an influential figure during my youth. Always a good friend of Mother's, she staunchly defended him, insisting he had never married because he hadn't met the right girl. My father, always loyal to Walter in public, used to tease Mother about him in private, saying he was light on his feet and that he wore lace on his underwear. Mother insisted Walter was shy.

What surprised me about Walter was that he talked about subjects other grown men avoided. He loved opera, antique furniture, good china, old silver, and fashion. Whenever he was with Mother she grew animated, and at times interesting. She felt timid around Father, whose robust physical and mental health she found daunting. But with Walter she truly came to life. He is one of the main reasons I did not want Mother moving to Toronto. Walter visits her regularly and, far more than I ever could, he keeps her in touch with the outside world.

He also has a keen sense of the ridiculous and a genial sense of malice lurks just below the smiling surface. He and I often play a game, planning imaginary publications, or drawing up a guest list for the party from Hell, or casting Wagner's *Ring* cycle with folk singers.

Catching sight of me, he smiled. "I'm glad to have you alone for a minute, Geoffry. I'm working on a screenplay. That's where the money is these days. However, and I am sure you will agree, I would like to avoid the trite. I was thinking of a film about a policeman who has been kicked off the force for being a renegade. He has become a private investigator."

"So far so good, Walter." If I had to force my good humour a bit it was due to my not having heard from Brian Fraser in twenty-four hours. He should have learned from the message that I was here at Mother's. The silent vacuum in which I found myself proved more unnerving than the threatening calls. At the very least I would know my stalker was holding a telephone and not out doing something dire.

My immediate task was to put Walter at ease. He continued. "Our private eye is a bit down on his luck, so he is sleeping in his office."

"That's a novel twist," I said. "Is he making coffee from three-day-old grounds?"

"How did you guess?"

"I'm psychic. Tell me, is he still in love with his ex-wife?"

Walter laughed. "I hadn't thought of that, but in it goes. He is suddenly accused of a murder he didn't commit, so he hides out in a motel with a large neon sign that blinks on and off right outside his window."

"Then he steals some clothes, which happen to fit perfectly, and he goes to a bar where the bartender is polishing glasses with a dishtowel."

Walter clapped his hands. "It gets better and better. I thought we might introduce a car chase in which he knocks over a fruit stand, only this time the oranges spill away from the camera."

"But only after he has stopped to give a coin to a blind beggar."

We were still chuckling when Elinor came into the room. "Would you like to see the table, Mr. Morgan? If I say so myself, it looks very handsome."

"Why I'd love to. He sprang to his feet with remarkable agility for his age and followed Elinor and me into the dining room. "You're using the Aynsley!" he exclaimed clasping his hands together with delight. "I helped Constance choose the pattern after she announced her engagement to Craig. It's as beautiful now as the day we picked it."

Walter was right. Ten gleaming green-and-gold bordered dinner plates sat flanked by two silver forks, a knife, and a spoon of a simple pattern to which age and use had added a soft patina. To the left of the forks lay heavy damask napkins, once white, now ivory with age, balanced by two wine glasses at each setting. For the crystal, I had been forced to mix and match. The keen observer would have noticed that the wine glasses at the two ends did not match the ones at the two rows of four settings facing one another down the length of the table. In the absence of flowers I had improvised a centerpiece from a cut glass compote bowl filled with grapes and tangerines. The sideboard had yielded four squat silver candlesticks which Elinor had buffed with a rouge cloth.

A Paul Revere bowl waited for cranberry sauce, and an Aynsley gravy boat, which had miraculously survived intact, would hold the giblet gravy. Slowly, Walter circled the table, reaching out to feel the surface of a plate, the texture of a napkin. He flicked at a wine glass with a fingernail to make it sing, picked up a fork to balance on the ends of his fingers, turned over the elaborately patterned ladle beside the gravy boat to examine the hallmark.

"The table looks remarkable, my dears. Good for you! This may well be Constance's last meal in her home. I'm delighted you are using all her good things." His mobile face turned pensive as he reached for the Paul Revere bowl and cradled it with both hands. "I gave this to Constance and Craig on their silver wedding anniversary. It does my heart good to see it used." Taking a spotless handkerchief from his pocket he buffed away fingermarks. Then he put a diminutive hand on Elinor's arm. "Just remember, my dear, never trust a person who does not appreciate beautiful things. Such people are anti-life, as what can make you feel more alive than beauty."

Our conversation was interrupted by the buzzer; the doorman informed me a Mr. Townsend was waiting in the lobby, and I rode the elevator down.

Larry was carrying a large bag. "I bribed two bottles of champagne from room service. They're still cold."

"I'm sure Elinor will be pleased. Leave them with the doorman and we can collect them on our way back."

We drove the short distance to Maple Grove Manor and pulled to a stop in front of the building. In a flash the doorman burst through the door. A queen from the grand old school of head-tossing, foot-stamping queendom, he wore his blue suit as though it were a uniform from a Ruritanian operetta, with gold braid, epaulettes, and a tall plume jutting from the cap. We have never spoken, only nodded, as I have heretofore left my car in the visitors' lot. As Larry and I stepped out of the car he bustled up. "I'm sorry, sir, but you can't park here."

"I'll only be a minute. I'm just going to collect my mother and she's not very steady on her feet."

"You'll have to leave the car over there, in visitors' parking, then bring it around."

Had there been a long line of cars and taxis pulling up to the front door I could have understood his concern, but the crescent-shaped driveway stood empty.

I remonstrated. "The entrance is not crowded and I'll be quick. I promise."

"I'm sorry, sir. Those are the rules."

Larry sidled up to the doorman. "If you let us park here I'll give you a blowjob," he whispered.

That did it. Checkmate. The doorman turned on his heel and stalked back into the building.

Mother is a creature of habit. Now that she is eating her evening meal at half-past five, she pours her first vodka as the four o'clock theme from *Sesame Street* bounces out of the television set. When I called to reassure her that I would be picking her up, along with my old friend Larry Townsend, who would take the other arm so she couldn't fall if she tried, I suggested that as she would be eating somewhat later than usual she might postpone her first drink for an hour or so. Far more involved with her television program than in my Christmas greetings, she murmured vaguely that yes, it did seem like a good idea and she would expect me shortly before six. She seemed curiously disinclined to talk, but she was probably suffering from a surfeit of Christmas cheer. I have it on good authority that Maple Grove goes in heavily for holiday trappings, gifts for all the residents, crackers and paper hats with meals, carols in the lounge, and holly everywhere.

To see Mother seated in her chair, dressed to go, a vodka at her elbow, was not unlike seeing a preview of a disaster movie about to open. It takes ingenuity to dress Mother. She must be propped upright so clothing can be dropped over her head, then seated so the rest can be pulled up from below. Mother has good clothes, but age has diminished her size and drained her of colour, so that she has the shape of an adolescent girl and the transparency of gauze.

Wisely the nurse had teased Mother into a long black skirt, meaning she could wear hose to the knee and flat shoes. A white silk blouse with long sleeves and a cascade of ruffles down the front added bulk to her pencil-thin frame. Already the ruffles were dusted with cigarette ash. She wore a pale gold wig, short and curly, like something copied from a Greek statue. An attempt to add colour to her pale beige face had turned it into a pentagon, two cerulean eyelids, two crimson cheekbones, one scarlet mouth. Poor Mother: a woman of unimpeachable virtue, she looked like a lady of the evening in retirement.

It was difficult to determine how much she had already drunk. I should have known she would not postpone her first drink very long. Leaving the warmth and security of Maple Grove took courage, and a vodka or two bolsters determination.

"Mother, you must remember Larry Townsend. We were at school together."

"But of course I remember Larry. I used to play bridge with his parents. How are you, dear?"

"Just fine, Mrs. Chadwick. Merry Christmas." Larry leaned over and planted a kiss on each cheek, carefully avoiding the red-for-danger rouge spots.

Taking both Mother's hands in mine, I lifted her to her feet, but not before she had polished off the vodka remaining in the glass. Larry helped her on with her coat, a fine black wool trimmed with sable, and each of us took one of Mother's arms and guided her out the door. She walked down the hallway as though it were the deck of the *Titanic* and stepped into the elevator as if into a leaky lifeboat.

"Do you want to press the button, Mother? When I was a kid you used to let me push the appropriate button on the elevator, or tell the operator which floor we wanted. Now it's your turn."

"Oh, Geoffry." She smiled quietly at the recollection and temporarily forgot her fear of elevators. As Mother, held up by Larry and me, left the elevator, the doorman moved to open the door. By a supreme act of will he bent his face into a grimace that could have passed for a smile. "Have a nice evening, Mrs. Chadwick."

Larry went through the door first. Still holding onto Mother's arm, he paused to give the doorman a long, lewd wink. We half carried, half walked Mother to the car and half lifted, half folded her into the front seat. A short drive along Sherbrooke Street brought us to Mother's building where, as luck would have it, the parking space I had found earlier had not been taken.

VIII

Alerted by the doorman, Elinor was waiting at the elevator as we stepped out. "Good evening, Mrs. Chadwick, I'm Elinor Richardson. I feel it is presumptuous of me to welcome you to your own apartment, but I'm so pleased you were able to join us."

"It's lovely of you to include me, my dear. I know Christmas is almost over, but I hope it has been a happy one for you."

As I ushered Mother through the door and went to put Larry's champagne bottles in the refrigerator, I felt distinctly uneasy, swept as I was with a kind of freewheeling apprehension. Seen from the perspective of the Grand Design, a group of prosperous English-speaking Montrealers was about to sit down to Christmas dinner, and fortunate to be able so to do. Seen in close-up, the situation afforded any number of opportunities for deviation from what is held by our tribe to be acceptable behaviour. We were a volatile mix, three generations and, according to some, three sexes. Add a few shots of liquor, a pinch or two of animosity, and stand back to avoid the flying shrapnel.

Walter Morgan floated out of the living room, borne on invisible currents of air, to greet Mother, kissing her soundly on both rouged cheeks and exclaiming how well she looked. Mother protested she looked a fright. I felt her version came closer to the truth. Walter and Larry shook hands, and Larry carried the coats down to Elinor's bedroom.

I steered Mother into her familiar wing chair and handed her a vodka on the rocks. Mildred looked disapproving, both at the vodka and my crew necked sweater, but she was obliged to smile as she introduced Alan, natty in a houndstooth suit, to Mother. Amy had also arrived while I was collecting Mother. She wore red jersey with a short skirt that on closer inspection turned out to be culottes. Black patterned stockings and high heeled shoes showed off her excellent legs, and she had taken care to outline her large dark eyes. She pulled a footstool over beside Mother's chair, and the two women smoked in tandem.

"I've found a kindred soul." Amy waved her cigarette. "We even smoke the same brand."

"I suppose we should all give it up." Mother spoke slowly and carefully, as though she had learned English as a second language. "They say it shortens your life, and it is a messy habit." Absently, she brushed away ash that had fallen into her lap.

"Not if you keep house the way I do." Amy took a sip of Scotch. "Do you know, Mrs. Chadwick, I once sent away for a subscription to *Good Housekeeping* and was refused?"

"Refused? Goodness me." Mother began to wheeze. She appeared to be having a seizure, but that is the way she laughs.

Amy stood. "Always remember that nature abhors a vacuum cleaner. Now, if you will excuse me, I'll go and see if Elinor needs a hand."

Walter carried an occasional chair to place beside Mother's and soon the pair of them were travelling backwards into the good old days.

My niece Jennifer and Elinor's son, Gregory, now arrived, said Merry Christmas, and went down the passageway to leave their coats. I went to the bar to pour myself a Scotch, where I was joined by Larry.

"Make that two," he said. "I went into the bedroom to get something from my coat and interrupted a triple X movie; your niece and the Bionic Man were giving one another a tonsillectomy. He'll have to spend the rest of the evening walking around in a crouch."

"They're the least of my worries. Mother is beginning to get animated. I only hope we can get some food into her before she checks out."

Elinor stuck her head around the kitchen door. "Geoffry, if you please."

I went into the kitchen. "How's it coming?"

"I'm tap dancing on Jello, but I'm managing. Would you lift the turkey out of the oven?"

I heaved the roasting pan on to the counter, and with the help of two large forks and a spatula we managed to lift the bird onto a platter.

"I'm supposed to carve that?" I asked with some dismay. "It looks as though it just escaped from *Jurassic Park*."

Elinor laughed. "Now, Geoffry, don't be a curmudgeon on Christmas Day. It looks just the way it is supposed to look."

Amy came into the kitchen. "Elinor, it's too much. You didn't tell me I was going to be having Christmas dinner with the cast of *Masterpiece Theatre*."

"Part of the cast," I added. "According to Larry, my niece and Elinor's son are smouldering in the bedroom where we put the coats."

"Damn them!" exclaimed Elinor. "They're supposed to be in the living room helping to make the party work, not necking below stairs."

"Leave it to me," said Amy. "Some situations require a delicate touch."

"And now," said Elinor, "I have to make gravy and steam the asparagus. Geoffry, would you do one more tour of duty and see everyone has a drink. Then perhaps you could uncork some wine. And don't hesitate to press Gregory into service."

I returned to the living room, where Mildred was spreading her own brand of anti-charm. In deference to the festive season she wore black, an elegant dress designed to show off her worst features. The square neckline, weighed down at each corner by diamond clips, showed off her angular collarbones and under-nourished bust. Women over fifty should cover up, unless they are overweight. Rounded shoulders and smooth collarbones are God's tradeoff for serious hips and a major backside.

She was insisting everyone open presents. Perhaps opening gifts wasn't such a bad idea as the aspect of theatre, the miming of pleased surprise and tiny explosions of gratitude, cancel the need to converse. Watching someone open a box of chocolates is intensely uninteresting, but no more so than social chat. Walter was helping Mother unwrap her gifts as her left hand was occupied with a glass, her right busy with a cigarette. At the moment they were jointly unwrapping the large bottle of vodka I had bought.

"Thank you, Geoffry, dear," she murmured. "Always useful."

"You told me you were giving her cologne," said Mildred, who still believes Mother is not too old to change her ways.

"I lied, and the other package holds cigarettes, not candy. So sue me."

Gregory and Jennifer came into the room, she looking flushed and pretty, he wearing his jacket open and holding his beer glass just below the belt buckle. They were followed by Amy, who tipped me a wink.

"All right, Geoffry, can I open the emerald necklace you bought me? Elinor spilled the beans. But you really shouldn't have."

"I'm afraid there's nothing here for you, Amy," said Mildred, who has zero tolerance for foolishness.

"Would you be a dear and give this to Geoffry?" Mother handed her glass to Walter as though he were a saint she was asking for intercession.

"Don't you think you've had enough, Mother?" demanded Mildred.

"Jennifer," I said, jumping into the awkward pause. "I could use a little help." The two of us escaped to the bar. "Will you take this to your grandmother," I said, adding water to the vodka. "And see if any other glasses need a refill."

Jennifer made a quick tour. In defiance of the season she wore a sheath of shocking pink shantung which enhanced her impeccable skin. Were I still a young man she would have turned my head, but nowadays an arthritic neck makes swivelling my head moderately painful.

"Amy would like a Scotch, and I'll have a gin and tonic, please."

"You seem to have taken a shine to Gregory," I remarked casually as I poured. Her smile was more than an answer. "He seems like a nice enough young man, well dressed, mannerly. I just hope his tattoos are correctly spelled."

"Oh, he doesn't have tattoos!" she exclaimed, artlessly springing to his defense.

"And how would you happen to know?" In spite of jeremiads to the contrary I still find the game of sex amusing. Caught out, what could she do but laugh with me.

"As I said, Jennifer, he seems like a reasonable young man, and he certainly is ornamental. My avuncular advice, for what it is worth, is to play it cool for a while. See him; sleep with him; but don't try to move in with him. Don't sew on his buttons and wash his dishes. Don't expect him to wash yours. Pay your own way. Think of all those pets you had as a small girl. If you chased them they ran away. If you walked away, they followed. End of lecture."

By way of reply Jennifer kissed me before taking Amy her drink. What is advice but a form of nostalgia, the wish to prevent those we like from making the youthful mistakes they are fully entitled to make. I suppose Christmas is as good a time as any to indulge in nostalgia, but perhaps I had better blame it on the Scotch.

The pile of presents under the tree had dwindled. "And this is for you, Alan." Mildred handed him a wrapped box with all the natural coyness of an armadillo.

I paused, curious to see what she was giving a man she had met only last night. I could tell Alan was uncomfortable; receiving an unexpected gift puts the recipient at a disadvantage, and he unwrapped the package gingerly, as though it might contain a crude practical joke. What it held was a letter opener in the shape of a tiny rapier, the hilt worked in damascene gold and silver. I had bought the knife for my father many years ago on a visit to Spain. It had no real value other than having sat on his desk until the day he died. I was astonished my sister could so casually give it away.

"I remember that," said Mother, drifting back into focus. "Geoffry brought it from Spain for my husband."

"Thank you. Thank you very much," said Alan, an innocent bystander caught in the crossfire. He put the box onto the floor beside the couch and covered it with the wrapping. The casually deliberate gesture suggested, to me at least, that he intended to forget the letter opener when he went home after dinner. I liked him the better for it.

"What's this?" asked Mildred, holding up a long, narrow box wrapped in red foil without a tag.

"That's for Uncle Geoffry," said Jennifer. "The doorman asked me to bring it up. Some woman dropped it off."

"A secret admirer no doubt," said Amy. "Let's hope she has good taste in ties."

To say I was swept with apprehension does not begin to describe the unease I felt. Whatever the package might contain, I did not want to expose it to the collective gaze of the room.

"Open it, Geoffry," ordered Mildred. "We've all shown you our presents."

"Can I get anyone a drink?" I stood and looked around, but not even Mother rose to the bait.

"I'll bet it's something naughty," continued Amy, "X-rated underwear, or a tie with a hand-painted naked lady."

"Probably handkerchiefs from L. L. Bean," I suggested with a leaden attempt to keep it light. Suddenly the room fell silent as everyone waited for me to open the last gift.

Bowing to the inevitable, I tore off the wrapping to find a plain box designed to hold a tie. Uneasily, I lifted the lid. Neatly folded inside lay a navy blue tie with tiny white polka dots. Underneath the tie was tucked a plain white card on which had been typed in uppercase letters:

WHERE DID YOU LAST SEE THIS TIE?

At first I made no connection. "It's only a tie, and a rather dull one at that." As I held it up to show the room I could see the tie had been worn. Faint creases in the light silk showed where it had been knotted. In a flash I remembered Brian Fraser reaching up to straighten the knot of this tie, or one very like it, just before I left his office. And if it was his tie, how come I was holding it in my hand? The implications were almost more than I could wrap my mind around.

"Is there a card?" asked Mildred.

"Yes, it's a joke present," I began to improvise, "from the wife of one of my colleagues. She once said her husband was too stingy to give me the shirt off his back, but that he might give me the tie from around his neck. And here's the tie."

"You need some new colleagues," said Amy. "And I was all revved up to be shocked out of my mind."

I hoped I did not look as green as I felt. "Well, if nobody wants another drink I think I'll get one for myself."

Once out of the room I hurried into the den and dialled Brian Fraser. "Hello. I am unable to come to the phone right now . . ."

I hung up with a queasy feeling that Brian might well be unable to come to the phone. Otherwise how did his tie, if indeed it was his tie, end up giftwrapped under Mother's tree? How had Dwayne Black, or his female accomplice, managed to get their hands on something Brian had been wearing? Could they have stolen it from his office? That was a possibility. Maybe he removed his jacket and tie to pull on a sweater when he went out on surveillance. Any other explanation did not bear thinking about.

I stood looking down at the telephone, irresolute. Ought I to call the police? If I did, what precisely could I tell them? That I had reason to be concerned for the safety of the man I had engaged to supervise my own safety? What had I to go on but an absence of communication and a necktie that may or may not belong to Brian. There was another caveat that caused me to hesitate. One of the reasons I had liked Brian all those years ago had been his strong sense of self-reliance. He refused to bow to the empty symbols of authority. Respect had to be earned. It did not surprise me that he had become a private investigator, in our North American mythology heir to the Western gunslinger living on the fringes of the law. Shane as Sam Spade. Were I to alert the police might I not risk offending him by officiously suggesting he was not capable of doing the job for which he had been hired? If I lost Brian's support by wounding his self-esteem I could end up right back where I started.

He who hesitates is reprieved. Elinor came into the den. "There you are, Geoffry. Would you please bring people to the table. Seat them as you see fit. Perhaps we should put your mother at one end. It is her table after all."

"Won't your place cards do the trick? I'm sure everyone here knows how to read."

"Place cards? What place cards?"

"The ones on the table. Didn't you put them there?"

"No, I did not." Wiping her hands on the bib of her apron. Elinor marched down the hall and into the dining room, me following. Facing each place sat a folded card embellished with a tiny snowman, on which was printed a name. To the right of the knife and spoon at each place lay a Christmas cracker garnished with a top-hatted snowman."

"Jesus H. Christ!" Elinor spoke softly, but with anger.

"Do I detect the fine hand of my sister? If so, let's reorganize the cards to suit ourselves. We'll leave the crackers. Fun for the entire family."

"Geoffry, there is no such thing as fun for the entire family unless the parents are too young to vote."

Mildred had put herself at one end of the table, me at the other, giving us the places indicating host and hostess. She had contrived to separate Alan and Amy, putting them on the same side of the table at either end, thus guaranteeing there would be no eye contact during the meal. Mother and Amy were seated to my right and left, no doubt so they could blow smoke at one another. Elinor was somewhere in the middle, below the salt, and not even on the side nearest the kitchen.

I placed Mother at the far end of the table, myself at the other nearest the kitchen. Elinor suggested she sit beside me, giving her ready access to the kitchen. Walter and Amy flanked Mother, with Alan beside Amy. Jennifer sat at my left, beside Gregory. I placed Larry beside Elinor, leaving one vacant place facing Alan beside Walter. By default it went to Mildred. She could talk directly across the table with Alan while Amy fondled his knee.

Elinor went off to deal with the asparagus and Hollandaise, and I went to collect Mother. After helping her to stand and give the ancient knees a chance to register they had changed position, I gently but firmly escorted her into the dining room and seated her at the far end of the table. Obediently the others followed, sorting themselves out according to the rearranged place cards. If Mildred looked disgruntled she at least had the good judgement to keep silent. She was obviously trying to make a good impression with Alan, and berating your brother over seating arrangements is not the way. I whispered a word to Jennifer who went off to help Elinor serve, carrying in plates of asparagus, steaming, fragrant, covered in golden Hollandaise. I poured white wine and brought Mother her vodka.

"Lift your fork, Mother," I said as Elinor slid into her place.

"Is anybody going to say grace?" asked Mildred in an attempt to gild her image.

"Grace?" echoed Mother, lapsing into consciousness. "We have never said grace in my house. If there is anybody who should be thanked it is Elinor, who cooked the meal, and perhaps the poultry farmer who raised the turkey."

"To Elinor," said Amy quickly, raising her glass.

"To Elinor!" we repeated in unison.

"Besides," said Amy picking up a stalk of asparagus in her fingers, "dead white males are history, and God is the number-one dead white male."

Mildred was not about to be stopped. "Let us drink to being together at Christmas," she began, her voice plummy with sincerity. "Here's to families – to friends – to roots."

Amy raised her glass. "To roots, and to the hairdressers who help us hide them!"

We ate.

Mother was having a wonderful time. Amy is an energy field, one who was not afflicted by the false reverence many affect when talking to the old. She and Mother smoked happily and chatted as though they had known one another for years. The conversation had turned towards gardening. Having lived all my adult life in apartments, I have had scant opportunity to learn whether my thumb is indeed green. Watering a potted plant is not a true test of gardening skills, although I once accidentally poured a pitcher of martinis onto a gloxinia, with unfortunate results. When Walter lived in a house, he had cultivated his garden, and his knowledge of the lore was extensive. Names like canna, campanula, clematis rolled easily from his tongue and certainly impressed someone like me who can recognize roses, peonies, lilies, and dandelions, even though they don't count.

"It's important to plant things like sedum," he was saying. "They last throughout the winter and give the garden a texture under the snow."

"I used to garden," said Mother, "but I could never keep abreast of the seasons."

"I once had a crack at gardening," said Amy, but when I found bugs on my plastic plants I knew I was in trouble."

"Plastic plants. Oh, dear me," and Mother dissolved into a wheeze of laughter. As she had eaten maybe three stalks of asparagus I was relieved when Elinor whispered it was time to carve the Christmas beast.

Large, golden brown, impregnable, the turkey lay on the counter sending out a silent, sullen challenge. At first I felt as though I were trying to carve through a knight in full armour, but once I got going the knife cut more readily. Amy and Jennifer cleared the table and waited to carry in plates of turkey, stuffing, mashed potato, and green beans, all miraculously cooked and ready to go at the same time.

We were an efficient team, me carving, Elinor serving, Amy and Jennifer carrying plates. In less time than I would have

thought possible we were all seated around the table facing
plates of food, the wine having been replenished by Gregory.
Gravy and cranberry sauce were handed around and a hush
descended, broken only by the soft clink of cutlery on china.

Turkey is not one of my favourite foods. Come to think of
it, I can't imagine anyone I know who would order a turkey
dinner given a choice, but so firmly entrenched is the tradition
that all across North America millions of families were sitting
down to the identical meal. That being said, as turkey dinners
go it was excellent. The bird was cooked just enough, the
stuffing was pungent and savory, the beans were crisp. About
the mashed potatoes I can find little to say other than they did
not taste like those served at summer camp. What impressed
me more than the food was the *mise-en-scène*. Elinor had
contrived to transform a frozen carcass and a mound of raw
vegetables into a traditional feast whose various ingredients all
came together at the appropriate time.

For a few moments the table was touched with grace. The
guests addressing their food appeared to be bathed in an amber
glow as we shared the secular communion of Christmas dinner.
If one person could be held responsible for making the evening
work it was Elinor, and beset as I was with private concerns I
could still admire and appreciate the effort involved.

Walter was speaking. He eats in such tiny bites that food
never seems to impede speech, and like many naturally grega-
rious people obliged to live alone he is stimulated by company.
I had casually mentioned that I had fallen asleep last night
watching *Don Giovanni*. For Walter, an opera queen of the old
school, that was all the opening he needed.

"Geoffry, I can't imagine falling asleep to the Don. Dozing

off during *The Marriage of Figaro* perhaps, particularly that end-less last act, but not the Don. Were you watching the Prague version or the Viennese?"

"Is there a difference?" asked Larry.

"Originally, yes. The Viennese version, staged in 1788, added a scene for Donna Elvira, a marvellous moment when well sung. She can really chew up the scenery. There was also a substitute aria for the tenor, who was not up to the demands of the original. Nowadays he generally sings both. In fact, the opera is usually performed uncut except for one duet, no great loss I might add."

"My husband didn't much care for opera." Mother paused while Amy lit her cigarette. "He used to call it 'grand uproar.' I love opera myself, particularly the one about the little Japan-ese girl who waits all those years for her husband in a Paris garret. Then when she learns he has married someone else she goes mad. It's very sad."

"Puccini was a brilliant man of theatre," continued Walter, "but Mozart created an archetype. Just imagine being at that first performance in 1787."

"I don't know," said Amy exhaling smoke, "there was a pretty good party going on in 1208."

Aware that he was losing his audience, Walter switched gears. "What brings you to Montreal, Larry?"

"I was en route to Florida and missed my connection. I forgot to leave a wake up call and overslept." Larry did not elaborate. He was keeping such a low profile that I could almost have been apprehensive. Yet so far he had kept both his drinking and his conversation well within acceptable limits.

"I used to go to Florida for a month each winter, but now

I'm too old to travel alone. And such of my friends as are still alive are not up to making the trip." Walter smiled, less from mirth than to muffle the note of self pity. "I've never been one to burn my bridges, but old age seems to have done the job for me."

"My husband used to say you must never burn your bridges before they are hatched." Mother picked up her empty glass, peered at the bottom and put it down, signalling me that she would like another.

While I was at the bar I heard Larry say, "Why don't you come down with me? I have a three bedroom condo in Lauderdale, one of those time-sharing arrangements which friends of mine are unable to use. That's a lot of space for one person."

Walter laughed a dismissive laugh. "If only you were serious, how much I could be tempted."

"I'm perfectly serious," insisted Larry. "We don't have to live in each other's pockets. I really like to have company over drinks and dinner, that is from six to nine in the evening. For the rest you can make your own schedule. I plan to rent a car. We could make some day trips."

"If you continue in that vein I shall be forced to say yes."

"Then it's settled."

As I put Mother's drink beside her ashtray I couldn't help wondering if Walter was really up to two weeks with Larry on holiday. I wanted the older man to return to Montreal in a seat in the cabin, not a pine box in the luggage compartment. Since I was already up, I inquired if anyone would like more turkey. Only Gregory volunteered. I suggested he bring his plate to the kitchen.

"White or dark?"

"Dark please, sir."

"I'm surprised by your mother, most pleasantly surprised. She has taken the most traditional of meals and given it flair. I'd call it a work of art, if that didn't sound too much like hyperbole."

"Mother is pretty together, but I don't think she could ever be an artist. You have to be unhappy a lot of the time if you're an artist, and she is too upbeat."

I thought it an unusual observation for a young man to make about his mother. Could it be that Gregory Richardson had a dimension beyond that of good looking jock engineer? I hoped for Jennifer's sake it were true.

"Would you like more stuffing?" I asked.

"Yes, please."

"I was at university with your father," I volunteered in an attempt to bridge the age gap that yawned between us. It turned out to have been the right remark.

"Were you really, sir? What was he like, back then I mean."

"I didn't know him well, but I remember he was good at sports, outgoing, a fraternity member, all the things I wasn't. I envied him because he was popular and I was not. Here, serve yourself to vegetables if you want them. Anyway, I had a friend who tried out for the football team. He was terribly disappointed because he was too small and was turned down. Your father took him out, bought him a few beers and persuaded him to try out for something else. It was a kind gesture, coming from the man who was one of the top athletes on campus. It was largely because of Andrew that I came to realize not everyone who is interested in sports is *ipso facto* a meathead."

Gregory laughed out loud. "I wish he could hear you say that." At the kitchen door he paused. "You've been very kind to Mother, Mr. Chadwick. My sister and I both appreciate it."

I gave a shrug and we returned to the dining room. By now the guests had split into conversational groups, making the occasion seem more like a dinner party and less like a directors' meeting.

Elinor smiled at me as I sat down. "The worst is over. The rest of the meal is cold and can be served anytime. This is when I can figuratively, if not literally, kick off my shoes."

Mildred stood. "I'll just clear away."

"There's no hurry, Mildred," said Elinor. "Jennifer and I will cope when everyone has finished eating."

"I don't mind, really." Mildred smiled at Alan as she reached for his plate.

"Please, Mildred," I said, "Gregory is still eating."

Reluctantly she sat. People like Mildred, and she is not alone, are forever painting you into corners, forcing you to make small social decisions and imposing behaviour you would sooner avoid. I did not enjoy calling her down in public; however, Gregory had not finished his second serving. I detest seeing plates whipped away before all have finished, as if cleaning up imposed a higher priority than enjoying the food.

The truly astonishing thing about Mildred is that she has a man in Toronto who wants to marry her. A colleague of her late husband, he seems, other than wanting to marry my sister, perfectly normal. I would have thought her about as marriage-proof as the Wicked Witch of the West, but on occasion I have to remind myself that not everyone has the good judgement to think as I do.

While Amy and Jennifer cleared the table I opened more white wine. As I circled the table, filling glasses, I wondered if I hadn't been unnecessarily apprehensive about the evening. More than just a minefield to be negotiated, the dinner party had turned into an event to be enjoyed.

Without in any way downplaying Elinor's prowess as cook, I found myself even more impressed by her ease as hostess. Somehow she had contrived to make this disparate group come together around a dinner table and give every indication of enjoying themselves. Furthermore, her guests were pairing off all over the place. Jennifer and Gregory sat enveloped in a cloud of crotch fog that only my niece's frequent trips to the kitchen helped dissipate. Larry had invited Walter to visit him in Florida. They made an odd couple, but if Larry had truly reached the point where dining with a congenial companion was better value than getting drunk in bars, he would have had to look far to find a more cosmopolitan man than Walter. Amy and Mildred were both trying to vamp Alan. I would have bet money on Amy, simply because she wasn't trying too hard, and her legs, in those lace stockings, were shown to great advantage as she waited table. Mildred was knocking herself out to be agreeable. If I, and perhaps Elinor, knew my sister was acting out a role in her own private scenario, we also understood she was therefore a more agreeable dinner companion.

My date for the evening was Mother. By now her Grecian curls were slightly askew and she had smoked away all her lipstick. A couple of times I had seen Amy, herself a seasoned smoker, move the ashtray just in time to catch Mother's elongated ash. Far from being daunted by the number of people, Mother was, in her own oblique fashion, having a high old time. The only strangers were Elinor, smelling like a rose since she had cooked the meal; Amy, a fellow smoker; Gregory, Jennifer's young man; and Alan, who seemed content to say little. If I had one major concern it was that Mother be swept with nostalgia for her apartment and wish to move back.

Uncivilized though it may sound, I grow restless at a dinner table; I feel caged by decorum. Using the pretext of seeing if Elinor needed anything, I escaped into the kitchen. Elinor was rolling out what looked like instant coffee in a plastic bag.

"My name is Julia Wilde and today we're going to prepare the three-minute dessert from Hell: vanilla ice cream, a generous shot of rum, a sprinkle of instant coffee powder, *et voilà*: *Parfait de crème glacée Elinor*. I had intended to serve a plum pudding – why break with tradition – but Mildred volunteered to buy it. By the time she went shopping yesterday afternoon they were all gone."

"Another triumph. Nobody will miss a pudding, believe me. Is there anything I can do to ease your path?"

"Yes, would you mind dealing with the champagne? The glasses are on the sideboard. Give me only a little. I don't much care for champagne; it's like drinking liquid heartburn."

"You and me both. I am convinced that if brides were toasted with single-malt whiskey the divorce rate would plummet. By the way, Elinor, I have to hand it to you. Dinner was bang-up, and Mother is having the time of her life. There's a lot involved, and I truly appreciate it."

"Thank you, kind sir. It's a pleasure to meet a man who understands meals don't simply appear with the wave of a wand."

"I'll go and pour the champagne," I said.

I have to admit that champagne is festive. The mere idea of

sparkling wine, like a bunch of helium-filled balloons, makes people smile. I eased out the cork while Elinor carried in the dessert.

"Would you like a little vodka, Mother?" I whispered, knowing her aversion to wine.

"I think I'll try a little champagne, dear, thank you. I haven't had it in years and it is Christmas."

I filled her glass, then circled the table. I suppose I should have served the ladies first, but I wasn't a professional wine steward and with ten people at table space was cramped.

"Shouldn't we drink to something?" asked Walter. "This is no ordinary wine. Someone should propose a toast."

"Larry," said Elinor, "why don't you give the toast. You brought the champagne."

From where I stood I shot Larry my laser look. He is no monarchist, but I have known him to toast the queens. Hesitantly he stood and raised his glass.

"I'm not very adept at this sort of thing, but let's drink to our two hostesses, Mrs. Chadwick and Elinor Richardson. And a Happy New Year to all!"

"Happy New Year!" we dutifully repeated, all except Mildred, who explained to Mother that as she was being toasted she wasn't supposed to drink.

"I guess it's our turn now, Mrs. Chadwick," said Elinor, raising her glass. "Here's to us!"

"To us," echoed Mother, who then aimed the glass at her mouth, drained it in three swallows, and passed out cold.

IX

Nothing throws cold water on a dinner party faster than having the guest of honour check out. Her wig askew, Mother slumped to one side, looking as though her bones had melted and only skin held her body together. For an anxious moment it seemed as if somebody had punched the PAUSE button, stranding us all in a particularly uncomfortable frame.

Elinor came to the rescue, rising to her feet as if it were the most natural thing in the world. "Why don't we take our champagne into the living room and stretch our legs before I bring the cheese out." She walked from the dining room, obliging the others to follow and leaving Mildred and me to deal with Mother.

"Shouldn't she be taken back to the residence?" demanded my sister.

"In this condition? Get real. We will carry her down to her room and you will put her to bed. Boys don't undress their mothers."

As Mother could not walk, I picked her up and carried her down the hall to the master bedroom. Even as dead weight she was easy to lift, so insubstantial had she become with age. Leaving Mildred to remove Mother's clothes and get her under the covers, I returned to the party. By now the guests had returned to their places and were beginning to open the

Christmas crackers. For the first time I was almost grateful to Mildred for having smuggled them into the dining room. Turning to your neighbour to tug the other end of the explosive tape, tearing open the cylinder, unfolding the tissue paper hat, and reading the joke or fortune on a slip of paper provided a diversion and helped salvage some of the festive mood.

As Elinor looked at me I gestured with my head towards the kitchen. "We have a slight problem." I began after she had joined me. "As you saw, Mother has passed out. If only Madame were here; Madame was wonderful at coping with Mother when she was . . . tired and emotional."

"I don't wish to seem nosy, Geoffry, but I assume this isn't the first time."

"Indeed not. This is one of the principal reasons I didn't want Mother to come tonight. She drinks more when she is excited. I was hoping she might make it through dinner, at which point I would have taken her straight back to Maple Grove. I suspect she had a couple of drinks in her room before I picked her up. Anyway, it's sleepy time down South."

Elinor began to unwrap cheese, Brie and Boursault for the youngsters, Stilton for the grownups. "Is she all right?"

"She's fine. As you suggested, this isn't the first time. The only cure is for her to sleep it off. Mildred is putting her to bed in her room. The problem is that Mother can't be left alone. Mildred will have to stay in your room. Would you mind terribly coming back to my apartment, just for tonight? There is a spare bedroom with a double bed."

"I don't have to put you out." Elinor arranged a wheel of crackers around each piece of cheese. "I can bunk with Amy."

"Think a minute, Elinor. Amy is twinkling at Alan. So is

Mildred, but she has lost by default. Justice is never poetic; usually it is harsh and retributive, but there is a kind of crude justice in Mildred being obliged to care for Mother when it was Mildred herself who insisted on bringing her here. Now, if Amy wants to cast her magic spell before Alan returns to Kingston, won't it be easier for her if you are not underfoot?"

Elinor looked at me in frank astonishment. "You surprise me, Geoffry. You are absolutely right. But why did you think of it and not I?"

"Because, my dear Elinor, way back when I was mis-spending my youth I learned to think of all the angles. Can I carry in one of these plates? And then I think we could all return to the dining room."

Elinor went into the living room to suggest we all have some cheese, and the party, minus Mother and Mildred, resumed around the table. Elinor and I were conspicuous in that we were the only ones not wearing paper hats. Amy was doing her best to keep spirits up.

"I'm very popular at Christmas parties," she was saying. "I can sing 'O come, all ye faithful' in Latin, and I know all the words to 'The Twelve Days of Christmas.' "

"I wouldn't put that on your CV if I were you," suggested Larry. "People have been deported for less."

"Watch it!" exclaimed Amy with mock severity, "or I'll sing the national anthem and you'll all have to stand."

Larry raised his hands in a gesture of supplication. "Let's compromise on 'Jingle Bell Rock.' "

By now a little bit tight, Amy began to sing, or rather bray on pitch: "Jingle bell, jingle bell, jingle bell rock!"

Mildred stalked into the room. I knew she was not a happy

camper. "Please, Amy, do you know there's an old lady asleep down the hall?"

"No," replied Amy, "but hum a few bars and I'll fake it."

For the remainder of the evening I moved onto automatic pilot, while the rest of the table settled gradually into post prandial torpor. Jennifer and Gregory, suspended in the glow of loving lust, could have been almost anywhere in the world, so absorbed were they in one another. Amy smoked and drank coffee. Aware that when she left Mother's apartment Alan would leave with her, she knew she had won. There was nothing to say, so, wisely, she kept silent. Too cross to converse, Mildred still managed to emit waves of ill will which intercepted mirth. Unless she could persuade Alan to remain, which seemed unlikely, she would have to sit tight while he went off with Amy. Walter and Larry got into an animated discussion over which of Garbo's films they would take to that hypothetical desert island, Walter arguing for *Camille* and Larry for *Ninotchka*. It was a silly argument, but it blocked out silence. Mildred brought the discussion to an abrupt halt by stating they were unlikely to find a VCR on a desert island. At that point Larry and I went to work on the brandy.

Walter looked at his watch. "Time for me to move along," he said from behind the camouflage of a smile. "We old folks need our rest."

I stood. "Not old folks, Walter, elderly gentlemen. Can I give you a lift? Taxis are scarce on Christmas night."

"That's very good of you, Geoffry, but the doorman assured me he can get a cab. I checked on my way in."

"It's no trouble, I assure you."

"No, no. I insist you stay. I don't want to break up the party."

Resisting the impulse to remark that Mother's abrupt exit had accomplished that, I tried to make a little joke. "Well, once you have left we can talk about you freely."

"You flatter me. If only I could believe I was interesting enough to provoke gossip I would leave a happy man."

We stood in the hall saying goodbyes. Larry took Walter's number and promised to be in touch the next day. After tiny explosions of gratitude, Walter headed towards the elevator.

"I think you will find him a very civilized person with whom to share a condo," said Elinor to Larry as she closed the door.

"I think he's a gas. I was almost depressed at the idea of going away alone, but now I feel quite different."

We returned to the dining room in time to hear Mildred say, "Well, Jennifer, we'd better think about tidying up."

The dining table had the look of controlled chaos which follows a feast. Crumpled napkins lay beside used dishes and cutlery. By now people had shed their paper hats, adding to the confusion.

Lest we be tempted to linger, Mildred began to tease the lace runners from under the plates. "I really must get these in to soak or the gravy will stain."

"Put them into Clorox overnight," suggested Amy. "Either they will come out squeaky clean or they won't come out at all."

Bowing to the inevitable, Elinor suggested we all move into the living room. Instead of joining us she went to her own room to pack an overnight bag, while Amy, Alan, Larry, and I sat drinking brandy. As my car was parked just outside the building I offered them a lift. Jennifer had been conscripted into helping her mother, and Gregory was waiting to take her home.

By the time Elinor joined us we were all ready to leave. Gregory went to fetch the coats. Jennifer came to say goodnight, but Mildred remained in the kitchen washing dishes by hand. I went to stand in the door. "We're just leaving. Are you going to say goodnight?"

"I already have. What time do you intend picking Mother up tomorrow?"

"I hadn't planned to pick her up. Can't you take her back to Maple Grove in a taxi?"

"She feels more confident with you to support her, and she hates cabs. Don't be late. I want to get to the Boxing Day sales."

Elinor came to stand beside me. "Goodnight, Mildred. I hope your mother will be all right. Don't worry about the fallout. I can deal with it tomorrow."

"You cooked the meal. It's only fair that I clean up."

"If you put the plates into the dishwasher with only a little detergent, I am sure they will be quite safe. And don't use the drying cycle."

Mildred did not reply as she reached for the gravy boat and emptied the remaining gravy into the roasting pan. Elinor gave a small shrug and left, leaving Mildred and me alone.

"Mildred, I've been waiting for a quiet moment to speak to you. I ran into Angus Fraser, although he now calls himself Brian. He asked after you."

"How is he?"

"Just fine," I replied, hoping that Brian was indeed all right. "He looks much the same, a touch of gray, a few more lines, but still tall and trim. His wife died last year. There are a couple of grandchildren in Halifax."

Mildred continued to scour the gravy boat.

"I have his telephone number. Why don't you give him a call next week. I'm sure he'd be pleased to hear from you."

Her hands slippery with hot water and detergent, Mildred lifted the gravy boat from the dish pan and fumbled it like a badly caught football. With a life of its own, it shot from her hands to hang, suspended, for what seemed like seconds, before plummeting to the floor. After surviving intact all these years it lay in shards at her feet.

"What a shame!" I exclaimed involuntarily as Mildred knelt to pick up the pieces.

She did not reply, and to my astonishment I saw she was crying. Mildred is not a woman who manipulates through tears. Even as a girl she only wept from genuine distress. For whatever reason – the smashed gravy boat, having been out-manoeuvered by Elinor and Amy, or lingering regrets over Brian Fraser, tears streamed down her cheeks. Perhaps I should have offered a reassuring word, maybe kneeling to pick up the pieces as I handed her a clean handkerchief. But Mildred is not an easy woman to comfort, and I knew she would sooner be left alone than subjected to sympathy. In this she was truly my sister.

I crossed to the kitchen table to pick up my corkscrew, and in doing so turned my back to Mildred, allowing her to weep unobserved. "I'll call tomorrow," I said as I slid the corkscrew into my trouser pocket. Without waiting for a reply I joined the others in the front hall. We said goodnight to Jennifer and Gregory, and rode the elevator down to the street.

As I unlocked the car door, to be met with the smell of cold vinyl, I decided to sit tight until tomorrow morning. If by then I hadn't heard from Brian I would try to contact someone else at his office. With any luck there would be somebody there, Boxing Day being less of a major holiday than formerly. Failing that, there might be a number on the answering service through which I could make contact with another investigator.

The night was still relatively young, and I knew it would be a long time before I felt like sleep. "Can I offer anyone a drink at my apartment?" I asked as I pulled away from the curb. "I have club soda for those who wish to avoid alcohol. We will not sing carols or pull crackers. In fact, we will do our best to avoid all mention even peripheral, of Christmas."

"Chadwick, you're a peripheral visionary," said Larry. "Count me in."

"A drink would be very pleasant," said Alan.

"Include me in," added Amy, sandwiched between Alan and Larry in the back seat. "I might even sweeten my club soda with a little Scotch. Are you sure you don't want to hear me sing 'On the twelfth day of Easter my true love gave to me'?"

"Only if I can recite *The Shooting of Dan McGrew*," said Alan. "For an encore I do Book One of *Paradise Lost*."

Amy let out a whoop of laughter. "You too can be as popular as the dog catcher. More important, Geoffry, what is your house policy on smoking?"

"Smoke as much as you like. Please use the ashtrays."

"That's a relief. Your sister started to cough as I was peeling the cellophane off the package. Thank God for your mother. I honestly think I'm too old to smoke in the bathroom."

We were all a bit giddy from relief at having Christmas dinner behind us, and the mood was definitely upbeat as we pulled to a stop in front of my apartment building. After letting the others out I took the car around to the garage, then went up to the lobby, one of those bleak architectural spaces designed to make a visual statement, not welcome the visitor.

The new doorman greeted me with a grin. "You missed a bit of excitement, Mr. Chadwick. The lights went out in the building. When the electrician showed up he discovered somebody had thrown the main switch. But everything's all right now."

"Very good," I said as I led the way to the elevator, hoping this Cheerful Charlie on the desk was temporary.

The elevator came to a stop and the door slid open. I led the way down to my apartment and unlocked the door. "Hang up your coats," I said as I turned on the light in the entrance hall. Tossing my own coat onto a chair, I flicked a switch to light up the living room and found myself facing a woman who stood in the middle of the floor holding a pistol.

"Good evening, Mr. Chadwick," she said in a resonant baritone. "I've been expecting you."

"Good evening," I replied, at a loss. "Mr. Black, I presume?"

"Right first time." By now Elinor, Larry, Amy, and Alan had come to flank me, two on either side.

"May I ask how you got into my apartment?"

"Easy," replied the intruder. "Your doorman couldn't keep a ten-year-old out of the building. All I had to do was cut the power, take the stairs to the second floor and wait for the lights to come on again."

"Ohmygod!" exclaimed Larry as the truth dawned. "It's Puff the Magic Drag Queen."

"In a manner of speaking," said the intruder. "I didn't realize you would be bringing friends home, Mr. Chadwick, but now it can't be helped. Why don't you all sit down." He gestured with the pistol. "Three of you on the couch, and the other two at either end of the coffee table. Please move slowly."

As we seated ourselves, Elinor on the camel backed sofa flanked by Larry and me, Amy and Alan in wing chairs facing one another, I realized how Dwayne Black had managed to get so close to me. His disguise could not have been more effective. In the gay subculture the word "drag" suggests flamboyance: big hair, heavy makeup, eyelashes like awnings, glittering fabrics, padded bras, stiletto heels. To cross-dress is to appropriate the symbols of femininity at their most theatrical. Dwayne Black had elected to disguise himself in street clothes, to dress for concealment rather than to attract attention. His short brown wig, two-piece navy blue suit, écru blouse with Peter Pan collar and medium heeled pumps could not have been more unremarkable or less deserving of notice. Such makeup as he wore served to soften his masculine features. As camouflage it was perfect. Small wonder he had been able to approach me unnoticed in the supermarket while I talked to Mildred.

"I know you're a bit weird, Geoffry," said Amy, "and I would be the last person to pass judgement, but is this your significant other, and if so, why is she pointing a pistol?"

"No, I am not his significant other," replied the intruder, who by now had seated himself on a straight backed chair facing us across the coffee table. "Am I to assume Mr. Chadwick has told you nothing about me?"

Elinor spoke. "No, nothing. And I for one would like to know why you are here. I am not accustomed to having someone point a gun at me."

"Before we get to story time," said Larry, "I was invited here for a drink and I really want it." He stood. "You can cover me easily while I go into the kitchen. Geoffry keeps his liquor over the sink."

"Please sit down," said the unfailingly polite Dwayne Black.

"And if I don't?" demanded Larry, more drunk than I had realized when we left Mother's apartment.

"Larry," Alan spoke quietly, "please do as he says." Reluctantly, Larry sat.

"I have to go to the bathroom," said Amy.

"It's just down the hall," I said. "First door."

Dwayne Black stood and moved to the right. "Move very slowly," he said to Amy. "And please don't do anything foolish. I'm a crack shot."

Amy rose and walked slowly down the hall. In the intense silence we heard the toilet flush. The door opened, and Amy returned to her place. "It's lucky I'm not French," she said. "Have you noticed how French girls can never go the bathroom alone? Now, what's the story?"

"I gave testimony that sent this man to prison," I explained. "I was in Toronto on business – you must remember, Larry – I was just about to enter a bank that had been held up by Mr. Black. He bumped into me on his way out and I was able to identify him to the police."

"Why couldn't you have minded your own business?" For the first time the veneer of politeness showed a crack. "What did it matter to you if I took a few hundred dollars? I was desperate."

"Weren't you breaking the law?" asked Alan.

"Whose law. I didn't make it."

"God's law. The injunction against stealing goes back to the Ten Commandments, and earlier." Alan spoke with the cool voice of reason.

"Because of his testimony in court I went to prison."

"I'm sure Geoffry gave his testimony under oath," said Alan, still travelling the high ground of common sense. "Had he not told the truth he would have perjured himself, thus laying himself open to criminal charges."

"That may well be so," continued our captor, regaining his composure, "But I was the one who was sent to the penitentiary. As you can see I am not a big man, so when I was surrounded by six of my fellow inmates in the shower, I was unable to defend myself. I was – excuse me, ladies – attacked. Four of them held me down and two of them raped me. It was an intensely painful and unpleasant experience."

Dwayne Black paused, as if to collect himself. "One of the men who raped me has since died of AIDS. He passed the infection on to me. One of the reasons I was paroled, aside from having been a model prisoner, was so that I would not die in the prison hospital."

There was a pause. We all sat silent, including Larry.

"The four men who held me down were in for life; they are still behind bars. One of my attackers died in prison."

"What happened to the other one?" Amy spoke for all of us.

"He died in a hit-and-run accident, crushed by a car I happened to be driving."

Had there been any question in my mind up to now, I realized beyond all doubt that Dwayne Black had come to kill me. That is, unless I could prevent him. The corkscrew I had slipped into my pocket before leaving Mother's apartment could serve as a weapon, were I able to pry it open unnoticed. It was not much of a weapon against a loaded gun, but it would have to do. Up to now I had been sitting straight with my hands folded in my lap. Trying to be unobtrusive without appearing furtive, I placed my left arm along the arm of the sofa and crossed my legs. At the same time I slid my right hand onto my hip.

"Well, that's one way of dealing with a rapist," said Amy. "Maybe it's lucky more abused women don't drive."

"Unfortunately, by the time the other four are eligible for parole I will be dead." Dwayne Black sat almost primly, knees together, skirt pulled down to cover them, the hand holding the pistol resting beside the other hand in his lap. "All of which leads to my reason for being here. I am going to kill you, Mr. Chadwick. Without your interference I would not now be dying."

The calm announcement brought an eruption of protest.

"Do you mean to tell us," demanded Elinor leaning forward, "that you intend to shoot Geoffry Chadwick, in cold blood, just like that? Let me point out that he was not the one who attacked you in prison."

"I believe there is an injunction against killing, somewhere in the Ten Commandments," said Alan. "Just thought I'd mention it."

While Elinor and Alan were speaking I slid my hand into my trouser pocket and attempted to pry up the end of the corkscrew, the forked piece that clamps onto the neck of the bottle, but it proved too stiff to move with just my thumb.

"Oh, well," said Larry giving a philosophic shrug, "if I had legs like that I'd want to kill someone too, only I think I'd probably kill myself."

"Don't listen to him," said Amy. "If you want to make your legs look good your shoes must match your stockings. Marlene Dietrich always said your shoes must be the same colour as your pantyhose to make your legs seem longer."

"Why don't you follow your own advice?" asked Dwayne Black. "Patterned stockings such as yours make any woman look as though she is suffering from the heartbreak of psoriasis, particularly someone who is no longer young."

"You could well be right," said Amy, obviously playing for time. "Of course if you really want to look tall and elegant, wear something long and dark, something that flows, with lots of movement."

"Like a river," added Larry. "I think he or she would look wonderful in a river – or a body bag. That's long and dark."

"You're beginning to get in my face," said Dwayne Black quietly.

"Cool it, Larry," I said. "Save the comedy for talent night."

Larry ignored me. "Look," he said to our captor, "if my oldest friend is about to be shot, I'd really like a drink first. Couldn't you cover me while I go into the kitchen and get a bottle of Scotch and some glasses?"

"Please stay right where you are."

"I'm old enough to drink. Would you like to see my driver's licence?"

"We live in a strange world," said Amy. "I was once asked to show my driver's licence to prove I was old enough to buy booze. It's like those TV ads that show people on vacation losing their travellers' cheques. They always seem to be on the beach or the golf course. Why do they need travellers' cheques if they're swimming or playing golf?"

"I have a question," I began. "It must have been you who left the giftwrapped tie with the doorman at my mother's apartment building."

"Hardly difficult to spot with your car parked outside."

I played dumb. "I may be a bit slow, but I fail to make the connection."

"I wasn't sure whether you would. It's a dreary tie. Your incompetent detective was wearing it the last time you saw him."

"I see. And where is he now?"

"Let us just say he won't be needing a necktie for the time being."

"Is he dead?"

"I don't know. He wasn't when I last saw him, only unconscious."

The situation was becoming more and more surreal. To sit around my living room table calmly discussing revenge murders as though we were talking about the current exhibition at the art gallery caused reality to shift. I felt like a tourist in my own life, watching from a distance as the scene played itself out. At the same time, my friends, demonstrating grace and gallantry under pressure, were playing the scene as though any minute the curtain would fall and we would retire to our dressing rooms.

"May I smoke?" asked Amy, to be met with an affirmative nod. "You know something, a man once forced his way into my house. He followed me home from a bar and wouldn't take no for an answer. I told him I'd give him twenty-four hours to get out. Do you know what he wanted to do? He wanted to cover my entire body with frosting – chocolate, from a tin – and then lick it off. I said to him, 'I want romance and all you can think of is food.' It just goes to prove that you can never trust a clean-shaven poet."

Elinor pushed the ashtray towards Amy. "It also proves that the way to a man's heart is through his ribcage."

"I was held up last month," said Larry, "all the way from the bar at the top of the Park Plaza back to my apartment. Never underestimate the power of the dry martini."

"Speaking of food, Elinor," said Amy, "that was quite a dinner you served up. Have you ever watched Elinor cook?" Amy addressed the question to me. "She actually tastes what she is cooking. Not me. If I tasted my food at the stove I'd probably lose my nerve to serve it."

"Another handy trick," suggested Larry, "is to buy your cookbooks at garage sales. That way they look well used. Very reassuring for the guests."

Amy and Larry were winging it, playing for time, trying to dam a spring flood with a wheelbarrow of sand. But all to no avail.

Dwayne Black stood. "I hate to interrupt this witty repartee, but this is not a social call. Mr. Chadwick, would you be good enough to step out onto the balcony. I would prefer not to shoot you in front of your friends."

"You don't have to shoot him at all," said Larry. "I'm sure he'd rather go to work than fax in dead."

"Your delicacy does you credit," said Alan. "Do you intend to shoot the witnesses? Are you going to kill the judge who presided at the trial? What about the police officers who guarded you in court?"

"I will not shoot you unless I have to. I would prefer to leave quietly and disappear. That will depend on you. Mr. Chadwick, if you please."

Alan moved very slowly to his feet. Holding his hands up, palms out, he spoke. "Can we talk about this? Surely you don't think you can break into someone's apartment and shoot him because you bear a grudge. This is Canada. It's Christmas. There has to be another way."

"You sound like Sunday morning TV. Sit down."

"Wait." In slow motion Alan took one step forward. "Think about what you are going to do. There are four witnesses. And if we are summoned to testify under oath we will be obliged to tell the truth, just like Geoffry here."

"You have to be alive in order to testify. And if you don't do as I say I may have to punish you."

"Oh, you masterful brute!" exclaimed Larry. "You're turning out to be my kind of drag queen."

Still holding his hands at shoulder height, Alan took one more step towards his antagonist. "Don't you know what the Bible says? 'Thou shalt not kill.' "

I knew Alan was up to something as he was not nearly so ingenuous as his remarks would lead one to believe. The same idea must have occurred to Dwayne Black, who took two steps backward. "Is that right. Perhaps you also know the passage in the Bible that says if you don't sit down – and now – I shoot you in the knees. Mr. Chadwick, come with me."

I stood and moved around the table. And then something happened that I will never forget. Elinor rose to her feet and came to stand in front of me. Wordlessly Amy joined her, followed by Alan and Larry, the four of them forming a human shield between me and my putative executioner. Partially concealed, I reached into my pocket for the corkscrew and held it behind my back while with my other hand I pried it open.

"Please sit down," said Dwayne Black with the exaggerated patience of a gradeschool teacher. "I won't shoot to kill, but a bullet wound can be extremely painful, especially in the knee. And remember: I have nothing to lose."

After sliding the corkscrew into my right hip pocket I edged my way between Elinor and Amy. "He's right," I said. "I don't want anyone to get hurt on my account." I moved towards Dwayne Black, who kept the pistol pointed at my chest. "I keep the door onto the balcony locked during the winter. Shall I open it?"

"Yes, please – and move very slowly."

I fumbled with the deadbolt which was stiff from disuse, and slid open the glass door, allowing a blast of frigid air to surge into the room. Dwayne Black motioned me outside with the pistol. My heart pounding, adrenalin racing, I stepped over the sill. The second I had both feet on the concrete terrace I reached for the corkscrew and spun around to catch my assailant during that fraction of a second when his attention flickered as he stepped over the sill. Swinging my right arm in a wide arc, I knocked the hand holding the gun to one side. On the return swing, I gouged the pronged lever into his face, raking it hard from temple to chin. With a cry he dropped the pistol. Pushing him hard out of the way, I managed to kick the weapon with my foot to send it skidding across the concrete and under the railing into space. Moving more quickly than I would have thought possible I ducked back through the open door and pushed it shut, throwing the deadbolt and effectively trapping Dwayne Black on the balcony.

Elinor was already in the kitchen dialling 911. Once the dispatcher came onto the line I fed her the address. I crossed the living room to the intercom so I could alert the doorman. As I waited for him to come onto the line I watched Dwayne Black standing with his back to the locked door. He reached up to pull off his wig and threw it onto the balcony floor. He kicked off his shoes. Bracing himself against the glass door, he hurled himself across the balcony and soared over the railing as if from a diving board. For a moment he appeared to hang suspended before plunging eighteen floors to land on a concrete sidewalk.

As I gripped the balcony railing and saw by the light from the street lamps the broken body of Dwayne Black I felt a surge of savage, shameful joy.

Amy was the first to follow me out. Glancing over the edge, she turned to go back inside and paused to nudge the discarded wig with her shoe. "Polyester, just as I thought. I knew it was too shiny for real hair."

X

With his quiet common sense Alan suggested he go downstairs to alert whoever was handling the body that the corpse was HIV-positive. Even as I pulled myself away from the rail I had decided to give up this apartment as soon as possible and maybe move to another building. Neither Elinor nor Larry ventured out onto the balcony; Larry almost tripped over his feet in his haste to pour a drink and Elinor admitted she was prepared to believe the man was dead without seeing the body.

The police arrived promptly, Christmas night being quiet. I told my story and urged them to put out an APB on finding Brian Fraser. All I could tell the officers was that he drove a dark blue Toyota, but they had means to trace the licence plate. Larry, who gravitates toward a uniform as iron filings to a magnet, wanted to ply the officers with Scotch. Being on duty, they refused. I assured them I had no intention of leaving the city and would make myself available at any time. By now the body had presumably been zipped into a bag and removed, most probably to the morgue. Finally, and to my immense relief, the police left.

We were a sober yet slightly drunken group as we sat around the table drinking neat whiskey from red-wine stem glasses, courtesy of Larry's spontaneous bartending.

"And that," said Elinor, "is that. Amy and I have always

stoutly maintained that never a favour goes unpunished. I invited you all for Christmas dinner and you ended up almost getting shot. I don't think this particular situation is covered by Emily Post."

"I for one am not about to indulge myself in ain't-it-awful." Larry paused to pour himself more Scotch. "A very unpleasant, not to say crazed, person came here to shoot my oldest friend. The friend was not about to go gently into that good night – thank you, English 100 – and decided to save his life. Upon which the unpleasant person, realizing he would be sent back to prison where he would die, decided on an unconventional but highly effective solution." Larry paused to drink. "I've seen too many people I care about die of AIDS to waste sympathy on a killer. If that makes me unchristian, so be it. *Ainsi soit-il*."

"You get no argument from me," said Elinor quietly.

"I'm glad he died," said Alan, "and I don't mean that vindictively. By his own admission he was a physically sick man, and on top of that drowning in hatred and malevolence. He wanted to take Geoffry out onto the balcony and shoot him, simply because Geoffry behaved like a responsible member of society."

"You had something in mind when you stood and started to move towards him," I said. "I was afraid you might get shot."

"I hoped to grab the arm holding the gun and make him drop it," Alan replied. "I have studied martial arts; I needed some way to siphon off anger when my marriage started to sour. I guess he suspected me, as he moved away – and not a second too soon."

"Thanks for trying to intervene," I said, "but I'm awfully glad you didn't take a bullet."

"I would have shot him myself when he made that crack

about my age and my stockings," said Amy as she lit a cigarette. "The moralists scoff at vanity, but it drives the world. Even sex is subject to vanity. As for hunger? People starve to bolster their self-esteem. You can steal my last dollar, okay; but don't step on my self respect. And – yes, I am deeply shallow. It's part of my charm."

We laughed quietly, less from mirth than from the relief laughter could afford.

Alan stood. "I think we should go. I'm sure Geoffry is exhausted, and even if he isn't, he needs to be alone."

"The doorman will get you a cab," I said.

"I'll walk," said Larry as he got up. "It will help to sober me up."

"You know something?" said Amy. "I had planned to spend Christmas alone. Then Elinor asked me to her Christmas Eve party, and to dinner. I met a whole group of new and wonderful people. I met Alan. I watched one of my new friends almost get himself shot. And I had a ringside seat for a suicide. It's been like no other Christmas I have ever spent. And I have to thank my good friend Elinor, who made it all possible."

"Words fail, Amy. Like Avis, we try harder."

During the business of putting on coats Amy drew me aside. "Elinor told me about your asking her back here so I could have the coast clear. You're a doll, a slightly alarming doll, but a doll nonetheless."

As we embraced, I whispered, "Can I assume you are too unnerved by recent events to spend the night alone?"

"I'm a total, absolute wreck, so much so that if he makes one false move, I'm his for life. But you haven't seen the last of me."

The moment had come to say goodnight. We were all strung out, pulled taut as piano wire, exhausted, and anxious to be alone, yet at the same time the events of the evening had forged a bond. We might separate physically, but we would be forever united by those brief, chilling moments when my life had been in danger.

Finally the gap widened. Amy, Alan, and Larry walked down the hall and onto the elevator. A flurry of waves and they were gone.

I closed the door and turned to Elinor. "Why don't I show you to your room. Perhaps you'd like to turn in."

"Not yet. Certainly not before we straighten up the living room. I'm far too hyped up and unsettled to sleep."

"Me too. I'm just beginning to realize how close I came to being shot. He was crazy but smart, a most unnerving combination."

Elinor shrugged as though ants marched down her back. "You're right about that off-centre mentality, very disturbing. To realize that the values we take for granted carry no weight. And yet," she smiled, "you kidded me about being ultra-Canadian and putting a good face on the fire at my apartment. You were being stalked by someone who wanted to kill you and yet you said nothing."

I too was forced to smile. "I guess you're right. What is more Canadian than a stiff upper lip. That and griping about the weather. I hate to think what might have happened had the others not joined us for a drink." I poured more Scotch into my glass. I would be sorry in the morning, but feeling hungover presupposes being alive.

"That's easy. He would have shot you from twisted motives

of revenge. Then he would probably have shot me so I couldn't testify. Not a pleasant thought. Maybe there is safety in numbers after all."

I took another long swallow of Scotch. "What really bothers me is that the rest of you were involved. To think I invited you all back in good faith only to have you threatened. I really hate it."

"You didn't plan the incident, Geoffry. And if it hadn't been for the others we might both be dead." Elinor put down her glass and came to stand in front of me. Resting her hands lightly on my shoulders, she smiled into my eyes. "Nobody blames you for what happened. I certainly don't. Larry treated the whole thing like a running gag. And Amy was at her histrionic best. What's more, we'll all dine out on the incident for the next year. So no more brooding."

Her smile was infectious. I smiled back.

"What you really need is a big bear hug," she said, "but perhaps you would prefer not to be touched."

"I'm willing to risk if it you are."

I put down my glass and wrapped my arms around her body, warm and solid. Her embrace was strong and infinitely reassuring. Her cheek, pressed against mine, smelled delicious. Never having been a touchy-feely sort of person, I hadn't been physically close, really close, to another human being since Patrick died. She felt good. I was a bit drunk.

I'm not entirely sure what happened next, but almost imperceptibly I turned my head to the left and brushed her lips with mine. She did not pull away. Our lips touched again, this time with slightly more pressure. The third kiss turned into the real thing as her lips parted to receive my tongue, tentative at first, but increasingly more insistent.

Gently but firmly she moved away. "I don't think this is a very good idea."

"You're right," I said. "I'd better stop."

"I didn't say I wanted you to stop. I only said I didn't think it wise."

"Wisdom is for the old." I kissed her again. She kissed me right back. Between the Scotch I had been drinking all evening and the events of the last hour or so, I was operating in overdrive. So, I imagine, was Elinor. There was no mistaking her enthusiasm. And although it was over thirty years since I had sexually kissed a woman, I discovered I still remembered how.

One of the few perks of age is that of no longer being obliged to play games. Taking Elinor by the hand, I led her down the passageway into my bedroom where we undressed and went to bed. Enough light filtered in from the hall to show me she had a heavy, well-proportioned body, lived in and comfortable. If she was a Maillol, I was more like a Giacometti as I, somewhat reluctantly I have to admit, peeled off clothing to expose my sixty-year-old torso.

As we lay down side by side I found my left arm trapped under her back. At once I was faced with the challenge, not unknown to men of a certain age, of having reached the point of no return and wondering whether I would be able to perform. I moved my lips across her shoulder and down over her left breast until I found the nipple. Whatever I was doing felt good to me and also to Elinor, as she half turned towards me. Even so, her right breast remained just out of reach, that is unless I wrenched my arm free. I continued to nuzzle the one I could reach.

"What's the matter?" she asked. "Don't you like the other

one?"

The tension broke and we both started to laugh.

"My arm is trapped."

She sat up, enabling me to free my arm and move into a crouch.

After giving her second breast its oral due, I moved slowly down over her abdomen. Kneeling between her legs I began to kiss and lick her vulva, moist, pungent, welcoming. She did not appear to mind and, more important, the effect on me was almost miraculous. I could not remember when I last had such an urgent erection, and in short order I was putting it to standard use.

For that particular kind of genital sex, women are extremely well constructed. It was so long since I had intercourse with a woman I had forgotten just how good it felt. What is there to say about a fuck that hasn't been said a thousand times in a thousand different ways. After a while sighs escalated into moans. "Oh, yes!" she cried out, and from down near the bottom of my spine I felt a pressure I could no longer resist. For the next few seconds things got a bit noisy and deliciously out of control. Then I was collapsed on top of her while she stroked the nape of my neck.

I can still remember from my dating days the tricky problem of what to say immediately after sex; what words does one use to coast back into reality after the ultimate in physical sensation.

Elinor spoke first. "I don't suppose you have any cigarettes, or chocolate bars, or nylons?"

"Excuse me?"

"Don't you remember how foreign girls during World War II would have sex for a package of cigarettes or a pair of nylons?

Mind you, this old grey head is no longer a girl, but we still have to make ends meet."

"Well, Elinor, there may be autumn in your hair, but there's still spring in your ass."

She laughed a loud, easy laugh. "That's the nicest thing I've heard since I moved back to Montreal. Geoffry, do you have any bread in the house?"

"Yes,"

"And mayonnaise?"

"That too. I've never done it with mayonnaise, but I'll try anything once. *De gustibus*, and the rest."

"That's not what I meant. How would you like a turkey sandwich? I sneaked some slices from the platter into my overnight bag, in Saran Wrap, I hasten to add. I could make sandwiches."

"Sounds good."

Moments later I was seated at my own kitchen table while Elinor, in a flannel nightgown trimmed in rickrack, stood at the counter cutting bread.

"Elinor, you've been cooking all day. Shouldn't I be doing that?"

"Not really. It's therapy. Between one thing and another it's been a very large day. What you could do is to pour us each a beer. I'll be finished in a minute."

Elinor set down the plate of sandwiches on the arborite surface and sat across from me. My bumsprung terrycloth robe and her flannel nightie made us look like an old married couple.

As if reading my mind she smiled. "Romeo and Juliet in middle age?"

"Hardly. More like Anthony and Cleopatra, only I'm the queen."

"I don't know about that. Either you have untapped resources, or you're one hell of a good actor."

Suddenly ravenous, I began to devour a sandwich. "Decidedly delicious. I'm seldom hungry at mealtimes and I was uneasy about Mother."

Elinor paused to chew. "I think it went very well, except for your mother falling asleep. Mildred got lost in the shuffle."

"There was a moment," I said, "just after we had served the turkey, when it all came together. I enjoyed a feeling of, I don't know, companionship, communion? For a few moments we were all playing on the same team. Unfortunately, it didn't last."

"It's not in the nature of those moments to last. They are ephemeral and for that reason must be seized when they occur, like our little detour into your bedroom. Even if it never happens again it was good while it lasted."

"Yes, it was." I made a wry face. "You have to admit, Elinor, I'm not much of a prize. *Pas un cadeau.* Even were I a grade-A heterosexual, I'm still a man of late middle years, set in his ways, unaccustomed to compromise. And – believe me – that is not your cue to jump in and list my three good points."

"Correction, five. And you can teach an old dog new tricks; it just takes time and patience." She smiled. "You have something very valuable to offer. In spite of your severe self-appraisal you possess the rare capacity to be a friend. I don't want a lover, not yet anyway, and maybe never. I still love Andrew. I want you to be my friend, with or without trips down the hallway. I can only hope you don't feel I am encroaching and crowding you."

"No, I don't. I don't think I can be a lover anymore, not for you, not for anyone. By that I mean the feeling of total absorption in another human being – in which my niece and your son are currently enveloped. You're old enough and smart enough to know the odds. And of one thing you can rest assured: my complete and absolute fidelity. If I'm not making it with you, I'm not making it with anyone. And it's not due to virtue or commitment or honour, but lack of wind."

We both burst out laughing. "I'll drink to that," she said, "much as I dislike toasts. You know something, Geoffry? Now that I have finished cooking that turkey and avoided being bumped off, I'd like to enjoy the rest of the weekend: movies, dinners, brunches, whatever."

"Sounds acceptable to me." I got up to pour myself another beer.

"And now, Geoffry Chadwick, I am going to bed in your spare room. No offense meant, none taken, but I don't know you well enough to sleep in your bed. The day has not been without incident, and I'm dead on my feet. Don't get up. I know the way."

Elinor came around the table, kissed me lightly on the lips and went to the spare room. I moved from the table and went to stand in the living room window. Outside stretched a tranquil cityscape punctuated by streetlamps. By now it was Boxing Day and what had been a most unusual Christmas had slipped into memory. I don't set much store on the afterlife, but were Patrick still a consciousness in a different, distant dimension I think he would be having a quiet chuckle. Imagine old Geoffry making out with a woman after all these years. I honestly believe he would also be pleased that the first person with whom I had been intimate since his death was Elinor, not a street boy or someone picked up casually in a bar.

I would have wished Patrick here so I could tell him, confess rather, to the shocking burst of elation I had felt on seeing Dwayne Black dead. That the reaction had been visceral and involuntary, like ducking to avoid a blow, did not negate the fact that it went against everything my family, my peers, my society had led me to believe in. But the reaction had been there, real and raw; and without Patrick there was nobody to whom I could admit what I had felt. Yet even as I regretted Patrick's absence, I realized with some surprise that my regret was tinged more with melancholy than with pain. I had begun to let go.

For Brian I could only keep my fingers crossed. The police were out looking for him; they had a description of his car. Dwayne Black had said Brian was not dead, only unconscious. Therein lay a glimmer of hope, faint, but a glimmer nonetheless. What was there to do but pray the police would find him while he was still alive. When I had definite news I would tell Elinor the whole story. So much had happened this evening I thought the footnotes could wait. And there would be time to tell stories, exchange experiences, trade confidences.

I turned away from the window and looked across the darkened room where so recently I had been threatened with death and rediscovered life. It is not in my nature to be gee-whiz optimistic, but I had to admit it felt good to be alive.

The following morning I awoke with a splitting headache and the jarring realization I had forgotten to take aspirin before I went to bed. I also had an acute case of the hangover hots, a recurring affliction during my thirties and forties. I took a pee and brushed my teeth, then went back to bed, uneasy about taking aspirin on an empty stomach. Soon I heard the toilet in the second bathroom flush, meaning Elinor was awake.

I slipped on my robe and knocked on her door.

"Come in," she called out.

"Are you in the mood for a visitor?"

"Only if your intentions are dishonourable."

I slid into bed beside her. This time there was no doubt about my ability to perform. Last night my cock had been attached to me, an integral part of my total physique. This morning I was attached to my cock, its insistent demands dragging the rest of me along, helpless and unresisting.

We fucked with silent, focused intensity. When we came, I thought my head would explode.

Cut to the kitchen where Elinor, by now aware of my fragile condition, scrambled eggs while coffee brewed. The bottle of aspirin sat beside the salt and pepper. We did not speak. There seemed to be no need, a state of affairs for which I was profoundly grateful.

Considerably fortified by the deftly scrambled eggs and a quiet buzz from the three aspirins washed down with black coffee, I took a long, hot shower. A shave and some casual clothes had me feeling better than I would have thought possible when I first opened my eyes.

A few minutes later, Elinor emerged from her room looking very pulled together, even though wearing what she had on last night.

"Do you remember," she asked, "the first time we had lunch and I was wearing what I had worn at Audrey's party the night before? At least I now have a decent excuse."

"It's the same excuse," I said striking a macho pose and

lowering my voice. "There was a fire that had to be put out. Excuse me. Did I say that?"

Hand on hips, Elinor glared at me with mock severity. "Yes, you did. I don't care if the manuals tell you to laugh at his jokes to bolster his ego; I'll pass on that one. Now it's time to pick up your mother. If Mildred wants to hurry out to the sales, I'll help you take your mother back to Maple Grove."

I moved closer to Elinor and put my arms around her. She returned the embrace. It was like the first time we had held one another last night, affectionate and non-sexual. For a few moments we held one another close, our bodies saying in a few seconds what speech could only approximate.

We put on our overcoats and I carried her bag onto the elevator which we rode down to the garage.

Both Elinor and I had keys to Mother's apartment, but we paused and exchanged a glance. I pressed the buzzer. After what seemed like a reasonable delay I rang again. Still no one came to open the door. I fitted my key into the lock and we stepped gingerly inside.

"Anybody home?" I called out to silence.

It did not take us long to discover the apartment was empty, not only empty but immaculate. All traces of dinner had been cleared away to the point one could almost have believed we had imagined the event. The leaves in the dining room table had been returned to the closet. Only a large plastic bag of trash in an otherwise gleaming kitchen hinted at last night's festivities. Leftovers, neatly wrapped, filled the refrigerator; the dishwasher sat empty. Further investigation showed us all of Mildred's personal effects had been removed from Mother's bedroom, and both beds had been freshly made up.

I had put down Elinor's case in the front hall, but we had not taken off our overcoats. "I think I'll run over to Maple Grove, just to see Mother is okay."

"Would you like me to come along?"

"Very much, if you wouldn't mind. I know Mother would be pleased to see you."

We drove to the residence, where I obediently parked my car in the visitors' lot. We entered the building – the archregal doorman was not on duty – and rode the elevator to Mother's floor. The door to her bedroom stood ajar. I tapped three times and called out, "Happy Boxing Day, Mrs. Chadwick. Are you decent?"

"Good morning, Geoffry. Come in, come in. And you've brought Elinor. What a lovely surprise."

Enveloped in a lavender robe across which marched nose-gays of violets, Mother looked surprisingly well, for Mother that is. She had obviously slept long and heavily, as her face had the freshly ironed look that proper rest bestows on the elderly. Shorn of her unbecoming wig, her face washed clean of the incriminating makeup, she looked like what she was, an old lady.

Elinor gave Mother a kiss on the cheek. "Good morning, Mrs. Chadwick, I hope you rested well."

"Very well, thank you, my dear. And I apologize for any inconvenience I may have caused."

"There was no inconvenience at all, I assure you. We all went back to Geoffry's flat for a drink and had a most interesting time."

Silently I thanked Elinor for not mentioning the intruder. To be comprehensible to Mother the story would have to be told with strings of footnotes and the result would only upset her. Better to leave her in the make-believe world where the sky is always blue, the grass forever green, and the robins go tweet, tweet, tweet.

Mother leaned forward. "Still, it was inconsiderate of me to put you out after all your hard work preparing that lovely meal. Suddenly I just wasn't myself."

Elinor reached for one of Mother's hands. "It is your apartment, Mrs. Chadwick."

"Not any more." Mother sat up straight, as if to pronounce *ex cathedra.* "I'm so glad you came by today, Geoffry, and you too, Elinor. I have reached a decision. I sat in the living room this morning while Mildred packed her clothes; she telephoned the station and was able to book a seat on the morning train to Toronto. It's a relief to have her gone. She does crowd one so. Anyway, I sat there thinking what better way to say goodbye to my home than with that lovely dinner and all those charming people. My last memory of the flat will be such a happy one. It would be a great mistake to return. I'm far better off here."

"If you really think so, Mother," I said dubiously, trying not to pirouette at the news.

"There is no question in my mind. Which brings me to my next point. Do you suppose I could have my wing chair from the living room? I had forgotten how comfortable it is. I will sit in it to watch television. Also, I would like my photographs from the bedroom. I do miss my photographs. For the rest, you deal with it as you think best."

"You're quite sure, Mother?"

"Quite sure, Geoffry." A nurse appeared carrying a tray. "And now it's time for my lunch. Thank you both for dropping by. I hope you will come back, Elinor."

"Next week, Mrs. Chadwick."

"So long, Mother. I'll pack up your photos and arrange for a mover to deliver your chair. Now we'll leave you to eat."

Elinor and I made a quick exit. "You see," she said as we rode the elevator down, "there are happy endings. I've always believed in them."

"It is a huge relief," I admitted. "She is far better off here at Maple Grove, but I wanted her to be convinced."

As we crossed to where I had parked the car, I paused and looked back at the building. "This is the future, Elinor, for me anyway. Will you come to visit me when I am in the sere and yellow?"

"Every other day and twice on Sunday."

"Twice on Sunday? That sounds like work."

"Not really. With your failing eyesight you won't be able to see me cheating at gin rummy. I shall win a small fortune which will help underwrite my own move to Maple Grove. I am not the first to have observed that life is cyclical. Now, with all the excitement, I forgot that I promised Mother I'd go for dinner tonight, so we'll have to postpone our movie. But if you can face another turkey sandwich I can give you lunch."

"With pleasure," I said as I opened the passenger door so she could get into the car.

"I love it when you're sexist," she said.

As I acknowledged her remark with a small bow I felt a great rush of something very like euphoria. Mother had decided to remain at Maple Grove, where her care would be in professional, competent hands. Such minor inconveniences that she must endure, such as fixed meal hours, were a small trade-off for knowing she was being monitored by those for whom looking after the old was a vocation, not a chore.

Mildred had returned to Toronto in a snit, but when I called to tell her about Mother's decision she would be mollified. And when I tell her I want her to come to Montreal, clear out Mother's apartment, and dispose of the contents as she sees fit, she will be overjoyed. I am well within my authority as Mother's attorney to delegate responsibility, and I will be spared the task of sorting through Mother's things.

Finally, I was grateful to Elinor for her company, the human presence that keeps thought at bay. The events of the last day or so demanded accommodation. I had to get used to the idea of living with what I had seen and felt. With Elinor no more than a telephone call away the period of adjustment would be eased. It was to begin with a turkey sandwich, and after that I would have to wait and see.

Epilogue

There's not much more to tell. The police grew immediately suspicious about a dark blue Toyota parked across and up the street from my apartment building with a parking ticket under the windshield wiper. After running a check on the license plate to find it registered to one A. Brian Fraser, they jimmied the trunk to find Brian unconscious and suffering from hypothermia. He was rushed to hospital and into intensive care. As soon as he is up to receiving visitors I will go to see him.

When he leaves the hospital I wonder if he will consider taking up another line of work. I engaged Brian to protect me, and by underestimating the determination of my adversary he succeeded in getting himself walloped over the head and me nearly shot. He too must have been taken in by the female disguise. One always has 20/20 vision in hindsight, but we were both seduced by bromides: Things aren't as bad as they seem; It can't happen here; People just don't do that sort of thing. The problem is that it can happen here and people do do that sort of thing. I must accept some of the blame for not having pushed Brian harder. I felt it beneath my dignity to appear unduly alarmed, to allow the stiff upper lip to tremble, and more-so in front of someone I knew.

And yet paranoia can be equally damaging. I do not want to turn into the kind of person who calls the police if he sees the police. Or as Larry once suggested: "Paranoia is when you suspect you are the only person in your office building who buys retail." Jokes aside, how does one walk the fine line between order and chaos without stumbling? I wish I knew. And whether or not the events of the past few days have made me a wiser man remains to be seen. On more than one occasion I have seen a bumper sticker that reads: "Don't get mad, get even." Perhaps the next time I read this message I won't manage to smile.

Some experiences do not ramify. I came close to being shot, but I wasn't. What more is there to say? Not too long ago I was nearly done in by a number 24 bus at the corner of Sherbrooke and University. Merely to remember makes me shiver. But I survived. I also got away with it on Christmas night. Perhaps the next time my luck will run out, but in the meantime, whatever remains of my life is there to be lived.

Sunday morning at ten A.M. I telephoned Elinor to find her cheerful and coherent. She told me that after what turned out to be an unusually pleasant evening with her parents, she came home early and went straight to bed. She also mentioned that Mildred had left an envelope on the dresser in Elinor's room. Inside was a one-hundred-dollar bill and a note. "Elinor, thanks for cooking the dinner. I hope this will cover my share of the expenses. M."

"I was pleased to find the money," continued Elinor, "not so much for the cash itself as for the gesture. I would prefer to like Mildred, or at least be on civil terms. After all, should Jennifer and Gregory stick it out and become a team I may have to deal with Mildred in the future."

"I suppose you are right," I said. "In the meantime, do you feel up to a workout? I thought I might go down to the club. Now that I have to meet increased demands on my energy it is more important than ever to stay in shape."

"La, sir, you bring a blush to me cheek. Actually a workout would be a good idea. I did fall upon the comestibles this weekend. Say in about an hour?"

Working out is not unlike having sex. You end up hot, sweaty, winded, and dying for a shower. Also, it is not necessary to converse. Elinor and I were puffing and panting when the weekend trainer, all teeth and shoulders, came into the cardio-vascular room. Elinor caught my attention in the mirrored wall and tipped me a broad wink. After he had gone out she spoke. "When I first joined the club Amy gave me a warning: No matter how cute your personal trainer, you can rest assured he's seeing someone else."

"True enough," I said, "and I'm almost certain that he and I don't read the same books."

After a companionable soak in the whirlpool bath, Elinor and I went to our respective dressing rooms to shower and change. In the foyer, I helped her on with her coat, held the door, and moved to the outside when we began to walk.

"And now," I said, "having soothed our consciences with exercise, we must partake of the four food groups: alcohol, sugar, fat, and caffeine. There's a restaurant only a couple of blocks from here that serves an excellent brunch. Shall we give it a try?"

"What a lovely idea! I've sort of overdosed on turkey." Elinor took the arm I proffered. "Amy called me this morning. Alan was still asleep upstairs. He has invited her to spend the New Year's weekend in Kingston."

"Good enough. Put two people together and the strangest things can happen. And speaking of strange, Larry called. He and Walter fell into a couple of cancellations, and they are off to Florida this afternoon."

"I feel a little bit like Dolly Levi," said Elinor. "Everyone is matched up except your mother and Mildred."

I smiled broadly. "Mother is paired up with Maple Grove – the Saints be praised! And Mildred has a perfectly respectable man who wants to marry her, if she'd only join the Earth People."

The restaurant came into sight. "And now, for the pause that refleshes, as Andrew used to say."

"Elinor, I am taking you to brunch on my liberated man's credit card, but I impose one condition, only one. When you are piling your plate with food I do not want to hear a single word about the diet you intend to pursue."

"I promise."

"As a matter of fact," I continued, "I recently read about what sounded like quite an intelligent diet, one you may wish to try when you and the rest of North America wakes up on New Year's Day and resolves to shed pounds. It's called The Valium Diet. You take three Valium before each meal and the food falls out of your mouth."

"I'll have to think about that one," she said.